Ace of Hearts

MYRIAD AUGUSTINE

JAMES LORIMER & COMPANY LTD., PUBLISHERS
TORONTO

James Lorimer & Company Ltd., Publishers acknowledges funding support from the Ontario Arts Council (OAC), an agency of the Government of Ontario. We acknowledge the support of the Canada Council for the Arts, which last year invested $153 million to bring the arts to Canadians throughout the country. This project has been made possible in part by the Government of Canada and with the support of Ontario Creates.

Cover design: Gwen North
Cover image: Shutterstock

9781459415027
eBook also available 9781459415010

Cataloguing data available from Library and Archives Canada.

Published by:
James Lorimer &
Company Ltd., Publishers
117 Peter Street, Suite 304
Toronto, ON, Canada
M5V 0M3
www.lorimer.ca

Distributed in the US by:
Lerner Publisher Services
1251 Washington Ave. N.
Minneapolis, MN, USA
55401
www.lernerbooks.com

Printed and bound in Canada.
Manufactured by Friesens in Altona, MB in May 2020.
Job #262267

To the Alvin that never got this story, and to all the other Alvins who have been waiting for it.

01 Woke Up New

"I HAVE LITERALLY *nothing* to wear, Meliss."

"Alvin, there's no *way* that's true."

Alvin rolled his eyes. He threw another shirt onto the growing pile on his bed, then fell back dramatically onto it.

"Okay, not *literally*," he admitted. "But everything I own is too boring or too safe or just too . . . *straight*."

There was a pause, and then Melissa asked carefully, "Isn't that kind of what we always shop for?"

Alvin's best friend wasn't wrong. At the small public school in Oakville they'd gone to, Alvin had always played it safe while Melissa urged him to be a little more . . . himself. They'd become fast friends in grade three, when their parents bought cookie-cutter houses on the same street. They both struggled with being outcasts. Melissa was bullied because of her weight. Alvin had been labelled gay by the other boys for all kinds of reasons he could never quite keep track of. The first time it happened was when Alvin said he was more interested in reading when everyone else wanted to play baseball. Then because they discovered he still played with a train set when he was twelve. Because he had tried to explain how suspension bridges worked. Once, because he had refused to snap a girl's bra strap.

The thing was, Alvin *was* gay. He just knew it had nothing to do with any of that.

Melissa had taken what other people tried to hurt her with and turned it into her armour. She was the first to call herself fat ("It's just a word!" she would say).

She wore what she wanted, when she wanted, whether it was a leopard print crop top in class or a bikini at the pool. The occasional asshole still tried to get a rise out of Melissa with an unimaginative joke. But she always laughed it off and responded with something far more cutting. Later she might vent about it, or cry if she needed to, but that was just between her and Alvin. Melissa was happy with who she was. More often than not, she used her reputation as a fierce fat babe to intervene when anyone was giving Alvin a hard time.

Alvin had never figured out how to own his outcast status in the same way. Maybe it was because everyone who accused him of being gay had such wrong ideas of what that meant. *He'd* known he was gay as soon as he learned the word for it, and had come out to his parents before he started high school. They didn't really get it either, but at least they cautiously accepted it. After grades nine and ten passed without Alvin bringing any boys home (or anywhere else), they seemed to conveniently "forget" that he had come out to them. They had even gone back to asking when he and Melissa were getting married. Alvin had planned to enter high school with a new sense of who he was: *out and proud*. But he had found himself surrounded by the same kids who were there in elementary school — and the same dumb jokes. Since there was no one who interested him, what was the point of being the only gay kid, except to invite more bullying?

Then everything changed again. Alvin's dad had gotten a job teaching at the university in Mississauga. Since Alvin's mom worked from home, the family had moved to be closer to the campus. It was hard to accept suddenly being two bus rides away from Melissa instead of a one-minute walk. But Alvin felt hopeful that this could be a fresh start in all the ways high school hadn't been.

"Hellooo, did you die?" came Melissa's voice. "All I can see is shirt."

Alvin sighed and raised his phone so that the camera wasn't buried in his chest. He could see that Melissa was, as usual, cycling through every filter. The current one — cartoon puppy ears and a wagging tongue — clashed with her carefully drawn eyebrows.

"Yeah, I know that's what I always go for," said Alvin. "I just . . . I don't know. Everything's going to be different. Maybe I want to be different too."

The words hurt to say out loud. Alvin's anger and embarrassment welled up along with the lump in his throat, and he quickly added, "God, that sounds pathetic, doesn't it? Like I'm some lost little lamb making my way in the big city. And it's not even really a city! Mississauga's just . . . a glorified suburb!" He let out a wordless screech of frustration, at himself and at the situation. Melissa laughed, and he couldn't help but laugh as well. "Our school had, what, two hundred kids? St. Salmerón's has *two thousand*. And it's Catholic. And I know *no one*. And —"

Mercifully, Melissa cut off this line of thinking. Her words reminded Alvin just why they were friends. "You're *not* pathetic. And you *don't* want to be different. You just . . . want to be more *you*. And this is the perfect time to figure out what that looks like."

Alvin barely had time to wipe his eyes with an old

T-shirt from the reject pile before Melissa continued. "Now, drag your sorry ass off the bed and point me back at the closet!" she barked. "I want to see that shirt I bought you for your sweet sixteen!"

Laughing, Alvin slid off the clothes-covered bed onto the floor. He ignored her usual crassness for a moment and gazed at Melissa through the phone.

"Seriously," he said softly, "what am I going to do without you around?"

But Melissa wasn't letting him slide back into despair. "I'm still going to be around. You've moved to 'Sauga, not Saskatchewan. Texts still work. Phones still exist. There are buses . . . usually. And once I get my licence, I'll be at your house every weekend."

Alvin rolled his eyes. "That's definitely not gonna make my parents stop hoping we'll get married." He stood up and switched from selfie mode. Melissa's face disappeared from his screen, but now she could see the few pieces remaining in his ransacked closet.

"No . . . no . . ." he heard her disembodied voice say. "Okay, maybe that shirt I got you is a *bit* too gay for your first day." He imagined her inspecting every piece before sliding the hanger aside. "Wait, hold up. Switch me back."

Melissa's face popped back up, with no filter this time. Her eyes narrowed suspiciously. "Alvin. Daniel. Persaud. Doesn't your new school have uniforms?"

As soon as she full-named him, Alvin flushed. He could never keep up a lie once Melissa caught him in it. He carefully tilted the phone so that she couldn't see the many McCartney's bags on his chair, holding a week's worth of button-up shirts and slacks.

"Well . . . yes, technically. But the first civvies day is the second Friday in. So I need to —" He held the phone away from his ear until she was done swearing.

02 Visions of Gideon

ALVIN HAD BEEN AT St. Salmerón's for less than two weeks, and he felt like quitting school forever. He was never the best student, but he wasn't the worst either. Plus, he expected that there would be a few adjustments. Half-size lockers. Religion class. Fast food served in the "cafetorium" — their word for the cavernous hall that did double-duty seating students for lunch periods and after-school performances.

What Alvin hadn't expected was to feel like he'd

been dropped into the ocean after growing up in a tank. The teachers had no patience for him, especially since he tended to get lost between classes and end up walking in late. With so many more students, Alvin figured he had a better than average chance of finding new friends, but instead . . .

WHUMPF.

Alvin was knocked sprawling out of his daydream, his phone skittering away under the nearest cafeteria table. As he sat up, wincing, he saw one of St. Salmerón's overgrown football players glaring down at him and wiping spilled soda from his jersey. The boy muttered something vague and threatening as he continued on. Alvin sighed and reached for his fallen phone, hoping the screen hadn't cracked any more . . . only for someone's foot to dart out and kick it away. He shot a look at the foot's owner. It was one of the other Caribbean kids at the school. Alvin had tried to befriend them, only to be called a "coconut" for his accent being too Canadian. The kid sneered as Alvin crawled forward. Just as he reached out again for his phone, another student passing by kicked it farther along. Alvin was aware now of the laughter running along the tables on either side of him. As always seemed to happen, he found himself the butt of a joke he wasn't sure how to escape. If he tried to reach the phone, they might keep kicking it. That would definitely damage the screen, not to mention prolonging his embarrassment until everyone got bored. If he left his phone on the floor, he was sure someone would steal it or break it, just for fun. Not much of a choice.

Just then, someone swooped in to rescue him. At least, that's how it felt to Alvin. Tall, with carefully messed brown hair, the boy ducked down to grab the phone while everyone else was focusing on Alvin's misery. The boy rubbed Alvin's phone clean on his vest and extended a hand to help Alvin up. Alvin took the hand gratefully, hoping that the blush burning the tips of his ears wasn't noticeable to anyone else. The blushing was partially due to the situation, but mostly because of who he was looking at. From the sharp cheekbones to the turned-around-but-not-quite-hidden septum ring, this guy was *cute*. Even though everyone dressed more or less the same, this boy's uniform was somehow a little more polished, and definitely tighter . . .

Alvin realized, with horror, that he was still holding the boy's hand, long after he'd risen to his feet. "Shit, I mean, sorry. I mean . . . thank you . . . for that." Alvin pulled back his hand as if it was burning. He turned to walk in the other direction and got about half a step before realizing his mistake. He turned around and held out his hand for the phone, all too aware of his sweaty palms. He hoped their wetness hadn't been noticeable during the unintentional hand-holding.

"Oh, no worries," said the boy. "Alvin, right? How are you settling in?"

Alvin blinked, not sure how to respond to what seemed to be a genuine welcome. He gingerly plucked his phone from the boy's hand. "Uh . . . not great. I mean, it's fine. I'm fine. How . . . how do you know my name?"

"Oh, I help out in the office, I saw your transfer. And I'm in yearbook . . . and student council. I know, it's a lot. I'm Alistair, by the way." Alistair extended his hand and Alvin shook it, laughing self-consciously. He blushed even more deeply as Alistair held on for a few extra seconds and winked at him.

"I'm Alvin . . . I mean, you know that. Obviously." Alvin was horrified at the words coming out of his mouth. He laughed again for lack of anything else to say. How could he be this bad at talking to another student? No wonder he couldn't make any friends.

Alistair didn't seem to notice. Or he was polite enough to pretend not to. "I'm *so* glad to finally meet you. I've gotta run — I'm coordinating the food drive for the Saints." At Alvin's blank look, Alistair chuckled. Even his laugh seemed polished. "The school's volunteer group? I know, the name's a bit much, but it's actually pretty cool. We do some really good work. You should check us out."

Alvin nodded, not trusting himself to say anything else. He returned Alistair's little wave as he watched him take off in the other direction.

Alvin was alone again in the middle of the caf.

The other students had moved on to more interesting things and, luckily, did not seem to have noticed Alvin's complete conversational meltdown. So Alvin was left with his original problem. He had no one to sit with, to talk about Alistair with, even to tease him about how he'd fallen apart at his first brush with a cute guy. No one here even knew that he would *notice* a cute guy. He looked over his phone. Luckily, it seemed unharmed, aside from a few new scratches on the case. That was good because he really needed it to work right now. Hurrying outside, he pulled up Melissa's contact. He knew she'd have her phone off during class, and waited impatiently for the voicemail to pick up.

"Meliss, can you skip last period? I need you to come to my house tonight. It's an emergency. I mean, wait, not like a scary emergency. No one's hurt. Except my social life. Which is already dead, I guess. Anyways, I need you to do me a serious social emergency favour." Alvin paused, then nodded to himself. He was committed. "I need a makeover."

03 Nails, Hair, Hips, Heels

MELISSA SHOWED UP THAT EVENING armed with a purse full of makeup, nail polish, and a stack of gift cards from her recent birthday. Alvin wasn't sure yet what he wanted to do, just that he had to do *something*. They planned and scoured the internet for examples as they rode the bus to Square One.

Swiping through Instagram, Alvin scowled. He finally shoved his phone back in his pocket in disgust. "It's no use. I'll never look like any of these people."

"We're not *trying* to make you look like them," reasoned Melissa. "We're trying to make you look like *you*."

"We're just going to waste all your birthday money!"

Melissa snorted and shook her head. "Are you kidding me? I've been waiting for the chance to give you a makeover for *years*. This *is* my birthday gift!"

She leaned in close and showed him epic makeover fails until he relented, laughing and pulling his phone back out. They huddled together, trying to figure out what would work for him and what wouldn't.

"Undercut," Melissa pronounced. She pointed a perfectly painted nail at the screen. "Definitely an undercut. That's like, the queer standard. And it's hard for a barber to mess up."

Alvin made a face. Before he could protest, she pressed on. "Go big or go home, right? You said when you called that you were having a social emergency. You can't deal with an emergency by going halfway."

Alvin took a deep breath, and then nodded. "I'm

thinking maybe my nails too? But I don't know what colour . . ."

Melissa thought deeply. Then a mischievous grin crept across her face. "I mean, why pick just one?"

Most of the looks Alvin and Melissa chose were a few thousand dollars and an airbrush or two away from what they'd actually be working with. But Melissa was a pro at getting eye-catching results on the cheap. And if Alvin wanted GAY — loud and proud and no mistaking it — Melissa was up to the challenge.

They picked out a few different outfits and some nail polish to round out Melissa's already impressive collection. Then they headed back to Alvin's house for the makeover.

By the end of it, Alvin was blazingly bright from head to toe — a different colour for every nail, the matching rainbow racer-back Melissa had given him for his sixteenth birthday, and a new pair of tight, black jeans she had insisted on splurging on. The mall didn't have much in the way of queer footwear, and Melissa had bellowed an increasingly frustrated

"BOOORING!" at every shoe store they'd searched through. But Alvin had come up with a fix for that. He carefully painted the aglets of his regular sneakers in rainbows to match his nails and top. It took a while, and it was so small that Melissa wasn't sure anyone would even notice, but Alvin was proud of the result. As they dabbed on each line of colour with tiny brushes, he thought of each aglet as a little pride flag that he could take with him everywhere he went. It was an undeniable statement, but low-key enough that it could be missed if he was in a crowded room or just heading somewhere on the bus. A very Alvin kind of statement.

Late that night, after Melissa had taken the last bus back to Oakville, Alvin stood in front of his mirror and grinned. He had been afraid with every change they made that he wouldn't recognize himself by the end of it. But the result was the opposite. He felt like he was recognizing himself for the first time. All that was left was to see how people responded to the new Alvin the next day.

The reaction to Alvin's new look was definitely . . . *different*. He couldn't tell for sure yet if it was a good different or a get-beat-up-after-school different. To be fair, the change was pretty extreme, especially in contrast to the black and white uniforms (what kind of school colour was *black*?) he'd had to wear up to that point.

"Oh my GOD, Alvin, you look *fabulous*!" a chorus of girls squealed in first-period history. They were girls who hadn't given him a second glance in the weeks before. People he'd never exchanged more than a sentence with complimented him in the hall. Even if he couldn't tell if the comments were genuine or sarcastic, it felt good to be noticed. It felt good to be noticed as who he really was.

Melissa had been sending him a steady stream of reassuring texts all morning:

u got this!

u r a babe!

ur here ur queer ur gonna do great

u owe me 4 hrs of sleep but u still cute

Alvin laughed at the last text and put his phone on silent as he headed to his Intro to Law class. Mr. Stanislaw always seemed to be in a terrible mood, no matter what anyone did. Alvin didn't want his good day to be ruined by drawing his teacher's attention with text notifications. As he rounded the corner, though, it seemed like that hope was pointless. Stanislaw was waiting by the door. As soon as he saw Alvin, he beckoned him over by crooking his finger. Alvin's heart sank. What could he have done wrong? He hadn't even stepped into the classroom yet.

"Mr. Persaud, a word," said Stanislaw.

Alvin gulped and dutifully stepped to the side. He wasn't sure why he was in trouble, but he didn't want to make anything worse by opening his mouth.

"Uniform code violation in your first month. Not

a good start." The gruff, balding man had a sing-song accent and a habit of mixing up his words. It made everything he said sound good-natured or amused, but his expression always showed he was anything but. Right now, he was glaring at Alvin like he'd set fire to a Bible. Some of Alvin's classmates were starting to gather near the door to watch the confrontation take place. A few even looked sympathetic. Alvin took strength from that and from his commitment to the new him. He decided to stand up for himself. Or try to.

"I . . . I don't understand, uh, sir. It's civvies day, so . . . no uniform? How could I —"

"There is still the uniform *code* when you are in the school, even when you're not in the school clothes. When we let you students pick what you want to wear, this always happens. Always problems."

Alvin flushed. He looked around, trying to draw Stanislaw's attention to the other students wearing questionable outfits that were just as daring as his own. Well, the straight version of daring. Before Alvin could say anything else in his own defense, Stanislaw thrust a sheet of paper at him. It was a formal violation slip, to be taken to and taken up with one of the vice-principals.

"I have called down already," Stanislaw said. "Miss Dougherty is in her office waiting. And I expect you to be caught up on what you are missing by next class."

With that, Stanislaw turned. The other students quickly ran into the classroom ahead of him before they could be marked late. Alvin started to follow, to continue to protest, but the door slammed shut in his face. He was left alone in the hall, shocked. He looked down at his clothes and then back at the paper he was holding.

"Great. Perfect. *Fabulous.*"

04 Cut to the Feeling

THE MAIN OFFICE HAD A ROW of ratty chairs covered with mystery stains. They stood against a wall of floor-to-ceiling windows, made of a kind of wired glass that Alvin thought was more suited to a prison. Everyone waiting to be seen in the office was on full display to the rest of the school. Alvin wondered if being shamed in front of your peers was supposed to make the judgment more biblical somehow. Or maybe the designers just hadn't thought there would be enough delinquent teens to require a separate waiting room. Maybe they had planned the window-wall to make the room less foreboding.

Alvin was pretty sure they had failed on that count.

Second period was a little too early for the usual troublemakers to get sent down. Even so, there was another student slumped in one of the chairs when Alvin arrived. Alvin found himself staring at him, his palms sweaty for the second time in as many days. Was there some kind of conspiracy to bombard him with crushes before he made even a single friend?

Alistair had been the very picture of school-approved handsomeness. Alvin was pretty sure he'd seen him in the McCartney's catalogue as a model. In contrast, this boy channelled an utter casualness, almost a disdain for where he was. His hair was messy, sandy brown streaked with remnants of bleached blond and a hint of blue fading at the tips. While Alvin's outfit might as well have been screaming his sexuality, this student's seemed to whisper it with a knowing look. He wore a faded band tee, grey jeans that Alvin was pretty sure were a brand made for girls, and a fleece-collared denim jacket with a rainbow peace sign patch on the shoulder.

Alvin took a deep breath, vowing not to repeat the train wreck of an introduction he'd had with Alistair. He walked across the room to hand his infraction slip to the woman at the desk. When Alvin turned back to take a seat, he found the other boy boldly looking him over. The boy didn't even bother to pretend otherwise when Alvin noticed. Alvin forced a casual smile, hoping it looked more natural than it felt. He sat down one chair away, searching his brain for something effortlessly cool to say.

"So . . . what'd they get you for?" was what came out.

Oof. Alvin winced as soon as the words left his mouth. It was dangerously close to dad-joke territory — all in less than ten words. He hoped that maybe one of their names would get called soon and put this conversation out of its misery before things could get worse.

"Smuggling, theft, arson. The usual," came the reply in a stage whisper.

Alvin laughed a little too loud, earning a disapproving look from the receptionist. But he was so surprised to receive a positive response that he forgot where he was. It was the first genuine laugh he'd had since he'd started school. Just like that, everything seemed a little bit brighter.

Changing to a regular voice, the boy continued, "Nothing serious, really. I miss classes sometimes. I bring a doctor's note. They send me here. I argue with the VP. I miss class because of it. They make me bring another note. It's a vicious cycle." He shrugged. To Alvin, he didn't seem to be overly concerned about spending so much school time in the office.

Alvin frowned, feeling like he was missing something obvious. "But . . . that seems . . . Isn't that a complete waste of time? Like, everybody's time?"

"Oh yeah, *huge*. But Dougherty's like that. She'll probably try to send you home unless you take off that nail polish, by the way."

Alvin held his hands out in front of him and looked down as if seeing the rainbow nails for the first time. When Melissa had come up with the idea, Alvin had been reluctant to go with something so noticeable. But now that he was faced with the possibility of having to get rid of them, he felt strangely defensive. "But . . . tons of people paint their nails. Students *and* teachers. Even on uniform days."

"Girls do, yeah," the boy corrected him. "And in normal colours. And not all of the colours at the same time. Not that I don't like yours," he added quickly, giving Alvin a reassuring smile. "It's just that's what some of the teachers here are like. Archaic." At Alvin's look of confusion, he added, "Old-fashioned. They'll say it's against the uniform code. But the uniform code *technically* doesn't prohibit boys from wearing nail polish. Just play the new kid card until Dougherty gives up. That's what I did last year, when I dyed my hair the first time."

"You're here to explain your absences, not to chat, Miss . . . ter Johnston-Grey. Rowan," a voice broke in. The voice belonged to a humourless and severe-looking woman dressed all in black. Alvin assumed this must be Vice-Principal Dougherty. He noticed the strange delay, as well. From the other boy's reaction, it wasn't an accidental slip, and it wasn't the first time it had happened. As Rowan stood and collected his bag, unhurried, he paused before following the vice-principal, as if she wasn't even there.

"If she's done with you before lunch," he said to Alvin, "you should go to the green room. Back behind the stage. You know where that is, right? Big thing, curtain, back of the caf, can't miss it?" When Alvin laughed, he continued, "That's where we hang out."

Alvin nodded, as if that made perfect sense, and then called out, "Wait, who's we?"

Without breaking step, Rowan pivoted on his heel, walking backward. He fanned his nails in front of him as if that answered Alvin's question, which provoked another sharp rebuke from Dougherty. Rowan rolled his eyes and disappeared into the vice-principal's office.

Alvin was perplexed. It was a strange meeting, but he felt hopeful that it was the start of something more . . . and not just a pity-invite to theatre club for the new kid.

05 The Velvet Rope

ALTHOUGH ROWAN'S INSTRUCTION to go "back behind the stage" had sounded simple, Alvin realized he had no idea what it meant by the time he actually got there. Standing in full view of everyone in the packed caf, trying to figure out his next step, he poked around behind the curtains. All he found were discarded props. He had almost given up when he heard laughter from somewhere stage left. As he fought his way through another curtain, he saw a door — and from behind it,

Alistair's voice rang out. "Come on, don't be mean. He doesn't *know* anybody. I think it was like he was . . . putting out the bat signal, or whatever."

Another round of laughter broke out after this. Alvin felt his ears burning as he realized they were talking about him. And his outfit. He was torn between the desire to interrupt them and figure out what Rowan had been inviting him to, or to run away before he heard anything else to make the day worse. He stood conflicted, his hand hovering over the door handle.

"Look, I'm gonna go get him, I'm sure he'd apprec —"

Too late, Alvin realized what was happening. The door swung open, bringing him face to (humiliated) face with Alistair, who could see he'd been listening. The taller boy barely let the surprise register on his face, though, before reaching out to pull Alvin into the room.

"*Aaaand* here he is, just like . . . I told him . . . to be. Right, Alvin?"

Alistair nudged him, and Alvin quickly played along. He nodded, taking in what Rowan had described as the green room. The first thing he noticed was that it wasn't green. Actually, the first thing he noticed was that Rowan wasn't there, but he didn't have time to be disappointed about that. The room was cramped and stuffy, with a couch jammed along one wall and an overburdened clothes rack opposite it. The door on the far side read STUDENT COUNCIL OFFICE. The room was barely large enough to hold Alistair, Alvin, and the three other students on the couch. They immediately burst into a chorus of praise for Alvin's outfit, which sounded especially insincere given what Alvin had overheard. Alistair rested his hands gently on Alvin's shoulders, angling him toward each of the three in turn as he performed introductions.

"Okay, first we have Robyn, like the singer, except they're, like, *way* more into sports."

A broad-shouldered student with thick boxer braids, Robyn gave Alvin a wave from where they were perched upside-down on the couch, their feet planting dirty shoeprints halfway up the wall.

"Then this is Wes. He's in band," Alistair continued. He turned Alvin very slightly toward the sullen-looking boy sitting beside Robyn, who stopped fidgeting with his spacers long enough to interject, "*Jazz* band." Alistair pretended not to hear him and pointed Alvin toward a girl with vampy red lipstick. She stood and began methodically inspecting each costume on the rack before throwing them aside with disgust. "And finally, Monica, to whom we owe our little hideout."

Alistair released Alvin's shoulders and edged through the room toward the far door. "Alvin, Trio. Trio, Alvin. Now, *I* have a student council meeting, but Alvin, I'm *so* glad you could join us." Before Alvin could say anything — thank you, goodbye, help me — Alistair was gone. With him, a pleasant lightness seemed to have left the room as well. Rather than finding a safe spot to hide from the rest of the school, Alvin felt as if he'd invaded another place he wasn't meant to be. The uncomfortable silence stretched on until Wes asked, "So did you, like . . . just find out you like dick, or what?" He snickered at his own joke until Robyn punched him in the leg.

"Sorry, Wes is a dick *nobody* likes. And he's a bitch about it."

Wes flipped off Robyn and their conversation quickly devolved into gross, petty in-jokes that Alvin couldn't follow. Monica shook her head and gestured for Alvin to come closer, saying, "Don't pay attention to them. They went out once, like, a million years ago, and it gave them Attention Deficit Dating Disorder or something." As she spoke, she lay gown after gown on Alvin's shoulder as if he were an extra clothes rack. She explained, "I'm trying to get Alistair into drag. I think he would look *so* fucking hot as a woman."

Alvin smiled uncertainly. He wasn't really sure how to respond but hoped that silent agreement would carry him to a part of the conversation he could actually contribute to. Monica scrutinized another dress, frowned, and threw it aside before asking, "Don't you think so?"

Alvin saw that Robyn and Wes were waiting for him to reply as well. His anxiety going into overdrive, he stammered, "Uh, y-yeah? I guess so?"

The three exchanged a look. Monica got a glint in her eye as she stepped closer to Alvin. "Oh yeah? You think Alistair's hot?"

"N-no? I mean, sure? If you think so?"

Just before Alvin was ready to throw down the costumes and run away, the Trio broke out laughing.

Monica laid a hand on his free shoulder reassuringly. "Oh my god, relax. We're just messing with you. Alistair's totally hot. If I was into guys, I'd want to do him too."

Wes and Robyn made exaggerated moans of agreement from the couch. Alvin's panic died down a little. He felt like he'd passed some necessary test, but he also felt a familiar weight in the pit of his stomach. He thought Alistair was attractive, absolutely. But that was as far as he'd thought. More than that . . . Alvin shook his head, pushing the thought from his mind and trying to pay attention to the conversation as it continued to swirl around him. Wes was arguing that someone named Jesse was a way better 'top' — a term Alvin was only vaguely familiar with.

Robyn rolled their eyes and groaned. "Ugh, *everyone*'s had sex with Jesse, though. He's so fake, it's . . . boring. His whole life is boring. Rowan is way more interesting. He's never around. I'm into the mystery."

Alvin struggled to keep up, every word adding to the weight. He always felt uncomfortable talking about sex. Plus, he was worried he would say the wrong thing and the Trio would revoke the approval he had just barely won. Alvin had felt something around Alistair, and with Rowan as well. But when he thought about what that might mean in the future, or what it would mean if one of them felt something for him, the details swam away from him. He wanted a boy to be into him, to want to be close to him. But whenever sex came up, it seemed like an additional complication. Alvin was still figuring out how to just talk to someone he liked.

Monica interrupted his thoughts, mistaking his look of discomfort. "Oh, don't worry, it's okay if people know you're gay or whatever. Some of the teachers are still, like, super religious. But this school's pretty chill. It's fine if you're out, and if people know you're hooking up. Just don't, like, get caught giving head in the bathroom. *Right, Wes*?"

Robyn and Monica both cackled. Wes went beet red, yelling, "It was *one* time! You've done way worse."

Alvin chuckled along with them, happy to let the focus shift to someone else and not have to explain his inner confusion. But Monica turned back to him right away. She slapped a hand to her chest, her eyes wide. "Oh my GOD, Alvin. We can totally be your wingmen!"

"Wing-gays," Robyn corrected.

Monica threw a pink feather boa at them before continuing. "Wing-*whatevers*. I guarantee, we'll get you laid by New Year's. Or at least *on* New Year's." The three of them laughed again, but the mention of the date was lost on Alvin. "So," she asked, looking at him expectantly, "What do you say?"

Alvin nodded, forcing a smile. "Um, yeah, that's . . . great. I mean, that sounds great."

"AMAZE!" Monica shrieked delightedly and clapped her hands. "Oh, you're *so* lucky you met us. We are gonna be your new best friends."

06 The Divine Miss M

SCHOOL BECAME A LOT EASIER to handle once Alvin had somewhere to hide and people to talk to. Though, to be fair, he didn't do a whole lot of talking. The Trio had their own dynamic that Alvin found difficult to keep up with, full of references to shared history or school incidents he hadn't been around for. And they had plenty of opinions they were all too happy to share. At length, and loudly.

They were also delighted to take Alvin under

their wing as a "baby gay" after he'd confessed to not having had any queer friends before them, or even knowing much about LGBTQ+ culture beyond what he'd seen on TV or online. Alvin was a work in progress, and they had a lot of ideas on how to work on him. Their first big project was a new (and less obvious) look for him to wear for the next civvies day. The month leading up to it passed quickly, and although Alvin was far from comfortable being the centre of attention, he appreciated being included. They'd hang out in the green room till well past the last bell. Alvin took to using the same excuse the Trio gave their parents — that they were volunteering with the Saints. They knew that Alistair would always cover for them if asked (though he never stopped insisting they should actually volunteer as well).

The night before his second civvies day, Alvin was walking home from the bus stop when he saw Melissa sitting on his front step. He realized guiltily that he hadn't texted her in days. She stood up and crossed her arms as he approached, looking him over. The Trio had sent him off in a mix of their own loaned items, clearly different from anything in Melissa's closet or Alvin's own.

"Hey, uh . . . everything okay?" Alvin asked.

Melissa raised her eyebrows. And then she exploded, just as Alvin expected her to. "Everything OKAY?! Are *you* okay? We agreed weeks ago I was coming over, and then you're not even here! And your parents aren't here! I've been sitting in the rain for an hour!"

Alvin winced as he fumbled to unlock the door. He let Melissa rage for a few minutes as they went into the house. Normally he would be showering her with apologies, but he just felt annoyed. Sure, he had been talking to her less and less as he'd been spending more time with the Trio. And sure, he had told her earlier in the month that he needed help with his outfit again. But shouldn't she be happy he had other friends, for once? Though . . . he hadn't really told her much about the Trio. He definitely hadn't mentioned Melissa to them. They were big on talking about how Alvin was now free from "hetero culture," and the number of jokes they made about straight people made Alvin reluctant to make

Melissa a target for them. It didn't seem like there was room in the Trio's version of gay for Alvin to have a best friend who described herself as "relentlessly straight."

"Look, Meliss, I'm sorry, okay? I lost track of time. And I thought you'd be at Jack's place."

He knew he'd said the wrong thing as Melissa's temper flared again. "Jack?! You mean Jacob? My *boyfriend*?"

Oops. Alvin knew how to deflect the anger this time, though. "Are we saying boyfriend? I thought all you did was —"

"Make out after drama class? Yeah, pretty much." Melissa laughed, and Alvin deemed it was safe to laugh along with her as she explained. "We got a *little* further than making out last Wednesday, though. So I figured we should have the relationship talk if we're gonna be having sex."

As they made their way to Alvin's room, Melissa went on, telling him about Jacob. But Alvin's brain was on two parallel tracks. He was happy she wasn't mad anymore, but he felt the usual discomfort around sex talk. It never used to bother him when Melissa told him about her conquests, but that was because he figured when he met a guy he liked, that discomfort would magically go away. He had always felt sure he'd be into it as soon as he found someone to be intimate with. But no matter how much the Trio guessed at his compatibility with Rowan or Alistair — or the much-talked-about Jesse, a boy Alvin hadn't even met yet — that discomfort remained. And hearing Melissa talk about her sex life just seemed to underline it.

Finally, she seemed to clue in to the fact that he was spacing out. She nudged him. "What about you? Get anywhere yet with *your* boy toys?"

Alvin made a face and shrugged. He stripped off the pieces the Trio had lent him (he and Melissa were long beyond any shyness about changing in front of each other). He laid them out carefully to wear the next day and pulled on a T-shirt and sweats.

"No, nothing," he admitted. "Alistair is this, like, hugely ambitious super student. He is always running between student council meetings, or running the volunteer programs, or some other extracurricular.

You know he wants to be the first gay member of Parliament for Mississauga?"

Melissa spun idly in the office chair by Alvin's desk. "That'd be pretty cool. You think he will be?"

"I don't think anything could stop him. But what do *I* have in common with someone like *that*? I couldn't even tell you what an MP does, much less how to become one."

Before Melissa could interrupt with her usual barrage of tough-love, confidence-building comments, Alvin continued. He spilled all the uncertainty he felt whenever the Trio talked about his dating prospects. "And Rowan is never around either, but . . . I don't know where he is, actually. Nobody does. It's this big mystery, and that just adds to how . . . I dunno, how *untouchable* he seems. He gets in trouble for skipping class or talking back and it just rolls off him. And whenever he is around, he's so smart about, like, queer history and politics and stuff. And the Trio just *swoon* over him. I could never be like that. I can't imagine we'd have anything in common either."

Melissa stopped spinning. She sat backwards on the chair and put on an expression of such phoney seriousness that Alvin chuckled without her even having to say anything.

"I know, I know," he said. "I don't need to be like them. I just need to be like me."

"I'm gonna make an app that tells you that whenever I'm not here. What's the other guy like?"

"Jesse? I don't know him. His family's super rich, so he hangs out with all the popular kids. He plays lacrosse. I don't even really know what that is."

"Ugh, he sounds boring."

"Yeah . . . except everyone's hooked up with him, apparently. Even the Trio."

"All of them? I thought Monica and Robyn were . . ."

"Apparently that's how Monica figured out she was a lesbian, after she and Jesse slept together at his New Year's party. Oh, yeah — Jesse throws this huge New Year's party that everyone tries to get invited to. And Robyn, they hooked up with Jesse on some overnight basketball thing, and it got *suuuper* awkward, which is why they don't do sports anymore."

Melissa made an exaggerated "impressed" face and they both laughed.

"Kinda sounds like he's a bit of a slut." She smiled. "At least that would make things easy for your first time . . ."

Alvin quickly shook his head, his stomach clenching at the suggestion. "No, I don't want to just . . . do it to get it over with. I told the Trio that, but they don't really get it. They think I'm just nervous about being with one of *these* guys, not nervous about being with *any* guy. They think they just need to make me more confident. They have a whole plan."

"I mean, maybe they're right." When Alvin scoffed, Melissa pressed on. "I mean, you're not exactly the most confident, Alvin! I love you, but you're not. And if they think they can help with that, why not try it? What do they want to do?"

Shyly, Alvin replied, "Well . . . they want to take me to the Village."

07 Colour by Numbers

ALVIN HAD HEARD OF "the Village" a few times before, but it seemed like something both mythical and historical, not a real place you could visit. The Trio had made the trip dozens of times and, with Melissa's prompting, Alvin decided to join them that Friday. Alvin had spent a few weeks laying the groundwork for the excuse he needed to visit Toronto on his own. His parents would never normally be okay with it — unless Alvin was joining the Saints downtown to bring food and warm clothes to the homeless. They knew he was about forty community service hours short of the forty hours he needed to graduate, so they were pleased he was finally taking initiative. Alvin felt a little guilty about the lie, but the guilt disappeared in his excitement at getting to explore the city. So, while Mr. and Mrs. Persaud thought Alvin was handing out soggy cheese sandwiches in front of some church, he was gawking at the sights along Church Street.

"I can't *believe* they closed down Crews *again!*"

Robyn's aggrieved tone broke through Alvin's wonder at being in the centre of Toronto's queer community. The Trio seemed at home, arguing about whether there was still a bar left that wouldn't card them. But to Alvin, every detail of the neighbourhood was new and fascinating. He kept catching himself staring at every gay couple holding hands, every stylish lesbian emerging from a store, every rainbow window decal proclaiming a safe and inclusive space. It seemed like a magical magnification of the cramped little green room they spent their lunches in. It was a bigger somewhere he could be surrounded by people like him, that was *dedicated* to people like him. Not exactly like him, though, Alvin noticed as they walked. Most of the faces he saw were white, and most of them in their thirties, and he wondered where the rest of "his" community was, if he couldn't find them here.

"I want to see if that little clothing store is still south of here," Monica offered as they paused at the corner of Church and Wellesley.

Wes quickly shook his head, replying, "Closed down. I think it moved to Kensington. We could see if that witchy place is still open?"

It was Robyn's turn to shoot down the idea, gesturing toward a storefront that had been converted to a condo showroom. "No, it used to be there. I think it was just a pop-up for last Halloween. Why don't we go to Glad Day?"

Finally, they mentioned someplace Alvin had heard of — and was interested in. Glad Day was the oldest LGBTQ+ bookstore still in operation, anywhere. For years Alvin had nursed a dream of graduating and moving downtown to work there. He would learn how to make latte art and maybe even bartend. He would join their collective and share passionate posts about local politics. When he had shared this plan with Melissa, she pestered him for weeks with book-related innuendo. But the dream hadn't died.

As they entered the store, Wes and Robyn broke off toward the café side of the space, while Monica wandered aimlessly among the bookshelves. Alvin didn't get more than a few steps in. He lingered beside the window display honouring "50 YEARS OF STONEWALL." He had a vague idea of what that was, how it had something to do with the first Pride Parade. He made a promise to himself to look it up later. The backdrop of the display was a collage of articles from the intervening decades, and Alvin regained the feeling of community that had evaporated as they walked through the Village. He could see bits and pieces of the neighbourhood as it used to be, faces barely older than his, people who had been arrested or beaten up for something as simple as being seen at the bookstore he was standing in.

Alvin felt humbled. He spent several minutes skimming the articles before turning his attention to the main exhibit. A dozen or so folded paper birds were suspended from the ceiling on fishing line to give the illusion they were taking off in flight. The lead and largest bird was painted in the rainbow colours of the pride flag. But Alvin was puzzled by the birds beneath it. Each one had a different set of stripes, three or five or seven, in colour combinations Alvin had never seen before. He figured they represented other communities, but there were no labels or explanations for the birds. He was embarrassed to ask the Trio to explain in case this was another thing they'd claim *every* queer person knew.

"I helped with those."

Alvin jumped a little at the voice. He turned to see that Rowan had snuck into the store behind him. The boy was grinning at having successfully surprised Alvin. Rowan pointed to the fourth bird down. It had sky blue wings and soft pink stripes flanking the white head and body.

"I folded that one," said Rowan. "They did a whole origami crash course workshop back in June."

Alvin smiled shyly and murmured, "It's beautiful. I could never make anything like that."

Rowan chuckled and shook his head. "Tell that to the hundred birds I crumpled up *before* I made that one. At least the paper was free."

"Not for the trees," Alvin quipped. He suddenly worried that the joke was too grim, ruining the light mood. Luckily Rowan laughed, so Alvin laughed too.

"Yeah, you're not wrong," said Rowan, nodding. "I guess being bad at art is pretty shit for the environment."

Alvin shrugged and leaned back against the doorway. From there, he could casually check where the Trio was, and whether they'd noticed him and Rowan together. They had regrouped at the back of the store and seemed engrossed in something else, so Alvin felt he had a few minutes of relative privacy. "I don't know. I think art's the one thing worth wasting paper for."

Rowan just smiled shyly, seeming at a loss for words, and they stood together in silence for a moment.

Turning back toward the birds, Alvin reached out and lightly tapped Rowan's contribution. It swung on the line, setting the entire paper flock swaying in opposite pendulum flights. "So, uh . . . what made you pick those colours?"

Again, Rowan didn't say anything. Alvin glanced back and saw Rowan's expression had changed to mingled confusion and skepticism, as if he thought Alvin was trying to trick him. "Because . . . it's the flag?" he finally said.

Alvin had no idea what that meant. He searched his brain frantically before deciding to go with the truth. "I don't . . . What flag is it?"

Rowan narrowed his eyes. When he saw that Alvin was truly lost, he gave a short bark of laughter that seemed to catch them both by surprise. "Sorry, I'm not . . . I'm not laughing at you, I just . . ." Rowan shook his head and started over. "It's the trans flag. 'Cause I'm trans."

Alvin felt the tips of his ears burning. He nodded automatically, as if it was obvious. It hadn't been obvious, not to him at least, and Alvin wasn't sure if that was good or bad. He had never met a trans person before, as far as he knew. He thought of a dozen different questions and internally silenced them all. He might seem naïve, or a little slow. But he preferred that to prying into Rowan's personal life.

"I . . . I didn't know. I mean, nobody told me. Not that I was asking about you. Or, like . . . would ask people if you were. Or . . ." Alvin trailed off, shrugging helplessly.

Rowan laughed again, and this time it was warmer and more genuine. "Honestly, don't worry about it, Alvin. Your not knowing was just surprising, given how everyone at school talks. I feel like that was the first thing everyone knew or wanted to know about me when I transferred. It's kind of refreshing."

Alvin nodded. He nervously picked at the edge of one of the peeling stickers in the window. "I think it's cool. I mean, not that it's a cool thing. Obviously, it's just . . . a thing, I mean. It's just who you are, right? It doesn't change anything. Between us."

Alvin winced at how every word out of his mouth sounded worse than the one before it.

Rowan playfully elbowed him and teased, "Oh yeah? Is there something between us that could change?"

Alvin didn't answer right away, unsure how to respond.

Rowan's expression became serious again. "You're fine, really. You didn't know. Now you know. It doesn't have to be a whole thing. Just don't be a dick or go all cis-martyr about it, okay?"

Alvin chuckled, finally relaxing. "Yeah, okay. Of course."

08 Body Talk

ALVIN FELT OUT HIS DEPTH. Seeming to know this, Rowan pointed to the other birds in the display, listing the groups that matched each bird's flag colours. Leather daddies, lipstick lesbians, bi pride, non-binary, ace, and demi. Alvin had never heard of half these things, or had heard of them only in bad jokes in old stand-up acts. He nodded, following Rowan's finger from bird to bird and trying to pay attention to the list of groups. It was hard, though. He kept stealing glances at Rowan, wanting to understand him even more than he wanted to learn about the display. There was something attractive in how patient Rowan was being, the knowledge he had and the way he spoke about it. He tapped into queer culture and community in a completely different way from the Trio. More matter-of-fact, more genuine, more relatable. At least it seemed that way to Alvin.

As if on cue, a chorus of familiar voices rose up from the back of the store, breaking into rude and echoing laughter. The other customers all looked up in annoyance. So much for Alvin's moment with Rowan.

Alvin angled his body slightly so that he could look down one of the aisles. The Trio had made their way to a bookshelf labelled *Erotica*, where they had each chosen a book. They were taking turns reading excerpts in loud and lewd voices that could be heard throughout the whole store. From where Alvin was standing, he could see more than one of the other customers in the store had made their way to the cash to complain. Alvin quickly excused himself, and rushed over to try to quiet the Trio down before they all got in trouble. At the same time, he raged silently at them for interrupting the connection he'd been having with Rowan.

Just as Alvin reached the Trio, he heard a stern voice from behind him that was clearly all out of patience.

"Listen, babies, I've told you a hundred times. Read the books, don't read the books, I don't care. But *don't* annoy the other customers. And *absolutely don't annoy me.*"

Alvin hated making a bad impression, and he hated the idea of making a bad impression at Glad Day more than anything. His dream of being a barista bookseller retreated even further. The clerk confronting them was tall and androgynous, with a heavily patched denim vest that matched the faded black of their jeans. Even as he squirmed with guilt by association, Alvin couldn't help but envy the aesthetic. It made the disapproval even harder to bear. Their Glad Day badge — identifying them as BREE, THEY/THEM — had a worn sticker stuck to the front. Alvin barely had time to recognize it as the ace flag Rowan had identified, whatever that meant, before he was shooed out along with the Trio. Rowan himself was nowhere to be seen. Alvin didn't blame him for disappearing rather than getting kicked out with them.

The Trio had been silent for the whole process, but their air of being scolded children vanished as soon as they were out on the sidewalk again. From the sound of the Trio's complaining, this wasn't the first time they'd been kicked out of Glad Day, and they didn't seem to have any intention of it being the last. Alvin trailed behind them as they moved on. He was caught up in the fear that he'd blown his chance with Rowan *and* any chance of getting to work at Glad Day in the future. It was only when Monica stopped and triumphantly crowed, "We're here!" that Alvin realized where their wandering had taken them. It was the attraction the Trio had been most excited to take him to, and the one he'd been most dreading.

Alvin looked up at the sign Monica was pointing at and his heart sank. A sex shop. Specifically, as the massive neon pink sign proclaimed, the *SEX SHACK*, complete with an inflated dancing condom in a lumberjack shirt. Under the questionable mascot, the windows were filled with displays of lingerie, bottles of lube, and furry handcuffs.

Alvin wanted to run in the other direction. But instead he let himself be pushed inside by the Trio as they chattered excitedly about what they wanted to get.

"Oh my *god*, look at this," Robyn exclaimed. They waved a comically large purple dildo at Wes, who pretended to faint. Alvin hoped that the size wasn't intended for actual use. Thinking about putting it in any part of his body made the usual nausea return twice as bad as when he saw the Trio in the erotica section at Glad Day.

Monica grabbed his arm. She steered him toward a table overflowing with different brands and flavours and sizes of condoms. "Okay, so," she said, grabbing a handful and shuffling through them like she was playing poker. "What do you normally get? I haven't had to use one of these since, like, grade nine."

Alvin was overwhelmed. He could barely focus on the table, and thought he might vomit all over it at any moment. He found some of the descriptions interesting, in an abstract sort of way. But even thinking about the actual act of putting one on, or putting one on someone else, was terrifying. He plucked one from the table at random and read the label as Monica waited expectantly.

"Ummm . . . strawberry-lime ribbed?"

She made a face, then shrugged.

Wes crowded in suddenly, taking the condom from Alvin's hand and throwing it back onto the table. "Oh, I would *not* recommend. Tastes way weird. And Jesse's, like, deathly allergic."

Robyn approached the table from the other side and started sifting through the baskets, unconcerned as they knocked some to the floor. They and Wes started bickering about whether or not strawberry allergies were a real thing. Monica made a face and pulled Alvin to another part of the store. A wall displaying a staggeringly large assortment of lubes loomed over them.

"Okay, forget that for now," she said. "What about lubes?" She threw a look over her shoulder at Wes and Robyn. Seeing they weren't paying attention, she lowered her voice before continuing. "I've actually never used any, though Robyn keeps saying I should. They got me a tingly mint one for my birthday, but it's *way* too intense."

Alvin fiddled with one of the packages, tempted to choose at random again. But Monica's hurried confession gave him pause. If she could be real with him about something like that, it felt wrong to lie to her.

"Um, I've . . . never . . . actually . . . used any either."

Monica's eyes widened, and for a moment she was speechless. Alvin didn't get to appreciate that rare occurrence for long, though. She loudly exclaimed, "Oh my *god*, Alvin, doesn't that *hurt*?! How do you even —"

Alvin gestured frantically for her to keep her voice down. He was afraid to look around to see if anyone else was paying attention. "No, it doesn't, because . . . I've never had sex."

"WHAT?"

This time, Monica's reaction was echoed by Robyn and Wes, who had become bored at the condom table and joined them in time for Alvin's confession.

Alvin sighed and closed his eyes. This was the last place on Earth that he wanted to be having this conversation. But there was no way around it now. The Trio was weirdly silent, waiting for him to explain. But he knew they could never be patient enough to wait until they all were somewhere more private.

Alvin let out a breath he hadn't realized he was holding. He opened his eyes and gave them a feeble smile. "Yep. Total, never-been-kissed virgin."

09 Goodbye, Yellow Brick Road

THE TRIO'S RESPONSE got them kicked out of the Sex Shack. This time, the clerk looked much less understanding. By the time they were back on the subway, the Trio had calmed down enough that Alvin could provide more substantial answers than just "Yes" and "Really." Alvin slumped into one of the scuffed-up red seats as the Trio crowded into the two seats opposite him.

"So," Alvin began. He focused his attention on

the random flashes of light in the darkness outside the subway car's window. "I wasn't out at school, so I . . . I never really got a chance to . . ."

Monica's hand shot up like she was in class, though she didn't wait a beat before countering, "But, like, *I* fucked guys before I was out."

Wes muttered, "Yeah, *loads* of guys."

This earned him a glare from Monica and a punch from Robyn.

Alvin started bouncing his leg nervously. Now that he had confessed one thing, he felt everything else he had been keeping inside struggling to be said out loud.

"I never wanted to . . . I mean, I didn't . . ." Alvin took a breath. "I've known I was gay since forever. I was never interested in doing anything with girls."

Monica sat back, contemplating this.

As if they were taking turns, Wes leaned forward. He looked skeptical. "But how can you have never done *anything*? No sleepovers? Summer camps? Hebrew school?" He and Robyn snickered at that last option, but Monica quickly shushed them.

"I just . . . it never happened. There was never anyone I wanted to, you know, do anything with."

This time, Robyn leaned forward. "Okay, hold up. If you've *never* wanted to do *anything* with *anyone*, how do you even know you're gay?"

This was the question Alvin had been most afraid of them asking. It was the question he'd never known how to answer, even to himself. He asked himself that question constantly, every time he felt the weight in his stomach, the uneasiness when sex was even mentioned in conversation. He knew he felt something when he looked at certain guys, when he watched certain shows or movies. He wanted to be with someone, in some way. But the details were hard for him to explain. Whenever Alvin saw himself actually being in a relationship — when he fantasized about Alistair, or Rowan, or even some vague idea of Jesse — there were dozens of little moments he could see them having together. Hanging out while they shopped, looking cute at dances, cuddling on the couch while they watched a movie. He wanted those things fiercely and deeply. And whenever he pictured these things, it was with a boy. But with anything more intimate than kissing, the fantasy went out of focus.

Without sex, though, what did that kind of moment mean? Was that just friendship? Alvin had done all of those things with Melissa, but he wasn't sure how to explain how they hadn't been romantic, when doing them with another guy would be. Could be. That it was different somehow, in some way he couldn't define.

"I guess . . ." Alvin's voice became unsteady and tears started to well up in his eyes. "I guess . . . I don't really know. I just —" He got too choked up to continue. He was angry that he was starting to cry, angry that he wasn't able to explain what he needed to explain. Angry that he had to be so complicated, so different.

Wes and Robyn shifted uncomfortably. They were clearly unprepared for this display of emotion, and said nothing as Alvin struggled unsuccessfully to regain his composure. Monica also seemed at a loss for words. But at least she reached over to squeeze his hand comfortingly.

They rode the rest of the way to Mississauga in uncomfortable silence.

The rest of October, and all of November, passed slowly. In a lot of ways, Alvin felt it was harder than his first week. At least before he had met anyone, he still had the hope of possible friends. Now he felt that he'd found the people he was meant to connect with . . . and they'd discovered he was a fraud.

The Trio hadn't actually said this to Alvin. He hadn't given them the chance to say anything after they'd returned from their trip to Toronto. He had avoided them at school the next Monday, then the day after that. Soon it had been weeks without a conversation lasting more than the occasional "hey" in the hallway.

Alvin spent his lunches and free periods haunting the library or out on the bleachers. He practised sketching. He played games or watched videos on his phone until he ran out of data, then went over his data. When Alvin's parents found out a week later, they grounded him, but that seemed redundant. He was already going nowhere, and talking to no one. He was busy punishing himself.

10 Good at Falling

ALVIN WAS SHIVERING out on the bleachers. It was the first actually cold day in an autumn that had been unusually warm. He was starting to regret the idea of keeping out of the Trio's way by hiding outside. That regret doubled when he realized that his lunch overlapped with lacrosse practice. The normally empty bleachers were scattered with knots of cheerleaders and other fans. It made Alvin feel even more conspicuous, sitting alone at the farthest edge. He squared his shoulders, trying to focus his attention more deeply on the video he was watching on his phone. But he wasn't immune to the main reason everyone else was watching the practice — the one and only Jesse Cabrera. The boy the Trio and everyone else seemed to be obsessed with.

Alvin had to admit, Jesse was definitely a babe, with thick wavy hair and dreamy dark eyes. It was clear that Jesse had plenty of admirers in the stands, boys and girls. And he blatantly flirted with both whenever he wasn't needed on the field. At one point, Jesse caught Alvin looking and gave him a wave. Alvin responded by slumping down and pretending he hadn't noticed.

With his head down and his sound turned up, Alvin really *didn't* notice when Jesse appeared in front of him a short while later. Standing the next level down on the bleachers, holding an icepack to his elbow, Jesse waved at Alvin again. This time, Alvin couldn't act like he didn't see him. He reluctantly pulled out his earbuds and faked a smile. He was not looking forward to meeting the superstar jock after all the stories the

Trio had told about him. He almost expected this to be a situation the Trio would deliberately set up to "help" his chances. But they were nowhere to be seen.

"Hey, Albert, right? Just transferred?"

Alvin grimaced, but tried to maintain the false smile. "It's, uh, Alvin actually."

Jesse shrugged, the correct name seeming to be an unimportant detail. He stepped up to the level Alvin was on. He sat down uncomfortably close and watched the remaining players continue practice. "Alvin, right, right. How are you liking Salmerón?"

It was Alvin's turn to shrug, as he edged slightly away. The question was a little too broad. He wasn't about to fill Jesse in on all the ups and downs of the last few months. For one, he doubted Jesse actually cared all that much about the answer. Second, he doubted he could relive all of it again without getting emotional. That wasn't exactly the stuff of a light-hearted first meeting.

"It's . . . bigger. More Christian. Feels weird for a school to have a chapel in it."

Jesse nodded the entire time Alvin was talking, but he never took his eyes off the field. "Yeah, pretty lame, you're right. But it's not bad once you get to know the right people."

This struck a little too close to what Alvin was struggling with. He had met the right people to make school bearable. Then he had ruined it by being too . . . complicated. Alvin made a wordless noise of agreement. Jesse was so set on running through his own script that he didn't notice Alvin's expression. In a way, it felt to Alvin like being back around the Trio. He had the sense that he was just bobbing along on the current of someone else's conversation. He could try to change the course, to swim upstream until he found something he cared to talk about. But it only made him exhausted, while everyone else ended up annoyed, or worse, oblivious. It was easier just to drift, to let others talk until they were done. But it wasn't very interesting.

". . . and my mom's gone most of the time, building orphanages in Africa or whatever, so I pretty much get the house to myself, which . . ."

Alvin nodded. And he muttered the occasional "yeah" or "for sure" as needed, to pretend that he was engaged. He let his attention wander out over the bleachers. More than a few people were pointedly pretending not to watch him talking with Jesse, but Alvin caught the side-eye and whispering. He hated to think of the rumours that would start, mostly because he knew the Trio would hear them right away. And the only thing worse than the Trio talking behind his back was not being able to get their advice.

". . . so we started throwing these seriously *epic* New Year's parties after grade eight grad. You should totally drop by. I'll introduce you to everyone."

It took Alvin a few seconds to realize Jesse had stopped talking and was waiting for him to reply. It took a second more to realize what he was expected to reply to. Jesse was staring at him intently, no longer watching the other lacrosse players. His expression was one of smug expectation, as if he was used to people responding to his invites with overwhelming gratitude. Alvin edged away again. Jesse had somehow closed the gap between them while he was talking. His knee was a distracting warmth against Alvin's own. Alvin briefly entertained the thought of just letting himself fall off the edge of the bleachers and out of the conversation. It would certainly be one way to avoid responding. Instead, he gestured vaguely with his phone and said, "Yeah, um, sure. I'll have to see what I'm doing, but . . . thanks."

Jesse looked stunned for a moment, as if it had never occurred to him that anyone would decline his generosity. Then he scoffed. "What *else* could you be doing? You just moved here, you don't really have —" He stopped abruptly, looking guilty. But the damage had already been done.

Alvin stood up, planning to finally make his escape. But he realized there was no quick or easy way to get past Jesse and down from the bleachers without making a scene. He dropped heavily back onto the bench, trapped.

To Jesse's credit, he looked genuinely apologetic. Seeing Alvin's desire to leave, he stood up himself and hopped down onto the level below. "Hey, for real. I didn't mean it like that. I don't think sometimes. I've just seen you sitting alone, I thought you were cute, and . . . I thought we could get to know each other better. That's all."

Alvin looked away, then nodded. What did he have to lose? Worst case, he would just stay home on New Year's Eve and listen to his parents complain about his cousins. He had spent the end of most years that way. He turned back to Jesse. "It's okay. Thank you. I'll try to make it."

Jesse beamed; the first real smile Alvin had seen from him. Alvin found himself warming up to the idea of spending more time with this boy.

11

A Thousand Forms of Fear

WHEN MELISSA'S CAT TIGER DIED, it was as heartbreaking to Alvin as it was to Melissa. As soon as she got Tiger as a kitten, Alvin had gone to his parents to ask for a cat of his own. He had been immediately denied for various reasons — their house was too small, his dad was allergic, they didn't think Alvin could handle the responsibility. Visiting Melissa's house was the closest Alvin had had to having a pet for the past eight years. So Alvin felt a bit guilty about not having visited Tiger since he'd changed schools.

After burying Tiger in Melissa's yard, the two of them went up to her room to reminisce. Alvin hadn't talked to Melissa since the day she had shown up at his house weeks before, even though he swore then that he would be more present. The truth was that he didn't want to relive what had happened with the Trio. He was afraid that explaining it would lead Melissa to ask the same question: How could Alvin know he was gay if he never thought about sex with a guy? Although he would never have wished for Melissa's loss of Tiger to be the reason, Alvin was grateful that they were back together, talking and joking like old times. Then he felt guilty again.

Melissa, perceptive as always to his moods, stopped her story and gave him a rueful smile. "This is nice. I missed it. I missed us."

Alvin nodded and swiped a hand across his eyes as he teared up. All of the unsent messages and unasked questions that had piled up over the last couple of months suddenly fought to be spoken aloud. So he explained it all. About the Trio and

Rowan and everything else. It spilled out in a rambling, disordered mess. He cried and laughed through most of it, and Melissa cried and laughed along with him. When Alvin was done, he fell back onto the bed, as if the act of remembering and retelling had exhausted him.

Melissa sat thinking for a few seconds. Then, without warning, she punched Alvin in the arm. Hard. As he yelped and rolled away, she dove in for another punch. Alvin held up a pillow as a shield until they both broke out laughing.

"That's for being a complete *ass* and not telling me about any of this!" she said.

"I know. I'm sorry, Meliss. It was just . . . a lot."

"It *is* a lot. I get it. So let's talk about it."

Alvin nodded. He rolled back over to Melissa and propped his head up on one hand. "I don't even know what to start with."

"Well, you've got to talk to Monica sometime. And . . . Robyn? And the other one."

"Wes. Everyone usually just says the Trio."

Melissa rolled her eyes. "Right. The Trio. Kind of pretentious, but whatever. They're not going to be *nearly* as judgmental in real life as they are in your head. Trust me."

Alvin made a face. Melissa pretended she was going to throw another punch, but just pushed him gently.

"I know, I know," Alvin admitted. "But what do I even say to them? About . . . the other thing."

"About what? Being gay? Come on, Alvin. You're gay. You know you're gay. I know you're gay. Ellen Page herself wrote me a letter *testifying* that you're gay. You're gay, end of story."

Alvin laughed. But despite Melissa's speech, he couldn't convince himself that everything would be fine. There was still one major obstacle that he had no idea how to handle. "I . . . still don't know how I feel about . . . sex, though."

"So? Sex can be good, or bad, or boring. Sex is whatever. You'll figure it out. They're your friends. And they want you to find someone that you want to spend time with."

"But then they expect me to have sex with that someone."

"And maybe you will! Look, Alvin." Melissa sat up. She waited until he looked her in the eye before going on. "Only you get to decide when you're ready. But you'll never figure that out if you don't give at least one of these guys a chance."

Alvin fell back on the bed again and hugged the pillow to his chest. He stared at the ceiling thoughtfully for a few moments. Then, coming to a decision, he sat up. "Okay, I'm in. Wanna creep their social media with me?"

Melissa rolled her eyes and dove to grab her phone from the bedside table. "Um, *always!*"

Building up the courage to apologize to the Trio took a few days. But Alvin finally found himself at the door to the green room (after another flood of supportive texts from Melissa). He thought about knocking, then

laughed out loud at how ridiculous he was being...
only for the door to burst open as soon as he laughed.

"ALVIN!" Monica and Robyn rushed forward
and engulfed him in an awkward, off-balance hug.
Wes hung back for a few seconds. Then, abandoning
any pretense of aloofness for once, he piled on to the
group hug that threatened to drag all four of them to
the ground.

As they untangled themselves, Alvin took a deep
breath. He prepared to launch into the apology he'd
been carefully rehearsing all week — only to be cut off
by the Trio's own overlapping apologies.

"Oh my god, Alvin, we were complete —"

"— I don't even know what I was thinking —"

"— and we talked about it, and it doesn't matter."

The three of them talking over each other was
so predictable, Alvin had to hold in a laugh while he
nodded and tried to pay attention to what they were
saying.

When it seemed they were getting to a point
where he could interrupt, he did. "Look, I . . . I still

don't feel like I'm totally ready for . . . other stuff. But my best friend, Melissa — you should meet her sometime. Anyways, she convinced me that I should at least go on a date. Or try to. So, as my *new* best friends, wanna help me out with that?"

The Trio screamed with delight.

Wes clapped excitedly. "Okay, well, we *definitely* need to get you invited to Jesse's party. He'll be there, obviously," he paused and shot Alvin a meaningful glance, "if you decide you're into him, I mean."

"And the party is the only time Alistair isn't running between a million different things," Robyn added. "So you can spend more time with him."

"And Rowan's invited. Though I don't know if he'll even show up," Monica finished. "It'll be the best chance to talk — or whatever — with all of them."

Alvin feigned a serious expression as they talked. He nodded in agreement until they moved on to scheming about how to get him invited to the party. Then he casually pulled out his phone and held it out to show them Jesse's contact info. "Actually, Jesse already invited me. Last week. We've been texting. *Aaand* he said I was cute."

The Trio screamed again. This time Alvin couldn't help but laugh out loud.

12 Expectations

THE LAST TIME ALVIN had been to an actual party, not just hanging out with Melissa in her basement, he was twelve. And he was pretty sure there had been a magician.

This time, there was alcohol, a massive stereo blasting music throughout the house, and an indoor pool. He got there an hour later than the Trio because he had to take extra care in covering his escape. His parents would never give him permission to spend the night at some rich stranger's party. Melissa knew how to handle it, convincing them that she and Alvin would be at her house, as usual. Instead, she was at her boyfriend's — a new boyfriend, Jacob already having bored her. And Alvin was in the fanciest house he'd ever seen. Everyone else in attendance seemed completely unimpressed, but Alvin was afraid to even touch anything.

"ALVIN!"

The Trio ambushed him just inside the . . . Alvin wasn't actually sure what to call it . . . front hall? Foyer? Jesse's mom's mansion had rooms Alvin had never needed words for before. Monica and Robyn quickly ran to his side and pulled him deeper into the house.

Wes ran off to the kitchen. Alvin could see through the open doorway that it was serving as the main bar for the night. Wes quickly returned with a couple rounds of shots for them all and a red cup full of something blue. "This was our contribution," he said. "Party punch. It'll help you catch up."

Alvin hesitated. Then he drained the cup in one go. After all, he was here, so he might as well commit to it. As soon as he swallowed, he started coughing, and the

Trio laughed. Wes plucked the empty cup from Alvin's hand and rubbed his back until the coughing fit passed, soon replaced by a pleasant warmth.

"Yeah, I wouldn't drink it that fast. It's mostly vodka and Sourpuss. But trust me, it'll really help with the nerves. And we *know* you're nervous."

Alvin tried to put on an easy grin, but it was true. He couldn't stop thinking about the main reason for him being there — to spend time with Alistair, Rowan, or Jesse. Melissa had told him to let things happen naturally, and the Trio had promised not to push him into anything he didn't want. But he had sworn to himself that *something* had to happen tonight. Otherwise what was the point?

Monica leaned in close and whispered, "There's Alistair. We're gonna let you . . . *mingle*." And before Alvin could protest, the Trio had disappeared, giggling, into one of the many rooms leading off the foyer.

Alistair wasn't exactly sober, either. His eyes were bright and his hair a little messier than usual. Alvin took a deep breath and jogged a little after Alistair to catch up before he made it to the kitchen. But Alvin found out that Alistair was a whirlwind outside of school as well. They had only talked for a few moments before he excused himself and flitted off to chat with someone else who'd just arrived. It wasn't exactly quality time, but Alvin was secretly grateful that he could start the night with something brief.

Alvin wandered through the house, intending to find the Trio and tell them how his first encounter had gone. He found himself in a cavernous room that contained the indoor pool, where Jesse was holding court. Surrounded by his usual entourage of rich kids and jocks that Alvin had never spoken to and honestly had no interest in ever meeting, Jesse was hard to approach. Still, Alvin stepped into the circle and ignored the looks Jesse's friends gave him at his boldly joining their conversation. Finally, Jesse noticed Alvin. To his credit, he moved away from the crowd so that he and Alvin could talk semi-privately.

"Hey, man," Jesse greeted Alvin. "I'm so glad you made it. Did you get a drink yet? I'll make you a drink."

Not waiting for Alvin to respond, Jesse led him to a bar set against the far wall. Judging from how expensive the selection looked, Alvin could see this alcohol wasn't part of the free-for-all in the kitchen. Alvin accepted the drink gratefully and, as Jesse waited for him to try it, took a sip and smiled. Rum and coke. It was probably a waste of fancy rum, but Alvin found it charming that Jesse went with something so basic, despite the lavish surroundings.

"Yeah, of course I came," said Alvin. "I wanted to see what everyone was talking about. Thanks for inviting me."

Jesse grinned and shrugged a little. "No big deal, really. Not like we're gonna run out of room."

Alvin laughed. Then, feeling a surge of confidence that might have been brought on by the alcohol in his system, reached out and laid a hand on Jesse's arm. "No, seriously. It was really nice of you to invite me. You've been really kind."

Jesse smiled and they held each other's gaze for a moment — until a loud splash and shouting interrupted them. Jesse's friends ran past. They grabbed Jesse and pulled him along with them as, one after another, they cannonballed into the pool in various stages of undress.

Alvin sighed with frustration. He had no interest in joining them in goofing off around the pool, and whatever moment he'd been having with Jesse was over. At least he'd tried. And hadn't embarrassed himself.

Alvin wasn't exactly sure what to do with himself. His instinct was to stick close to the Trio. But he didn't want to reinforce the idea that he was the lonely outsider with no friends, even if it was kind of true. He drifted from room to room as he finished his drink, marvelling at the décor. He was surprised at the number of other guests who recognized him, or at least pretended to recognize him, from shared classes or just passing each other in the hallway. A few of the other students, Alvin belatedly found out, had taken to calling him "Rainbow" on account of his first civvies day. He wasn't sure if he liked the nickname or hated it. He had never really had a nickname that wasn't an outright insult, and he had to admit he'd leaned pretty hard into stereotypes for that outfit.

Eventually, he ran into the Trio again in what he would have called the living room in a normal house.

That is, if he hadn't already wandered through two other rooms with couches and TVs bigger than anything his parents could afford. This time, the couches had been pushed back against the walls. About a dozen kids were standing in a loose circle. He recognized Alistair in earnest conversation with one of Jesse's lacrosse teammates, a lanky girl with a bob haircut who was so tall that even Alistair had to crane his neck to talk to her. In the middle of the room, Robyn and Wes were trading a massive (but mostly finished) bottle of vodka back and forth while a few others encouraged them. Staggering a little after draining the last drops, Robyn carefully placed the bottle on the floor and gave it an experimental spin. Everyone in the room gave a cheer.

Realizing what he'd walked into, Alvin groaned. He tried to back out of the room, but Monica appeared at his elbow to intercept him. Grinning, she pulled Alvin forward with her, shouting, "First spin is *Al-viiin!*"

13 Blue Lips

AT MONICA'S ANNOUNCEMENT, everyone cheered again. Alvin didn't recognize half of them and doubted they had known him by name before that moment. He would have bet money that they were drunk enough at this point to cheer anything. Even Alistair was considerably more relaxed than when Alvin had seen him last. He seemed to have taken full advantage of the open bar and the joints being passed around. His lips were stained the same blue as Alvin's from the punch. Alistair waved at Alvin and gestured to the space next to him as people began to sit down. But Monica steered Alvin to a spot on the opposite side of the circle. She sat down heavily beside him and traded a full cup of punch for his near-empty one. She explained in a not-so-quiet whisper, "It's a *lot* harder to get it to land on the person next to you, trust me." The kids on either side of them giggled. Alvin took a big gulp from his drink to hide his embarrassment.

Monica nudged him and, setting down the punch, he leaned forward to take the first turn. Alvin had never actually played Spin the Bottle before, but it seemed pretty self-explanatory. He had seen it done in movies and on TV. He reached out, grabbed the narrow end of the bottle, and spun it hard. A little too hard, as it turned out. The bottle continued to spin for several long seconds. Alvin nervously waited for it to stop, half hoping it would land on Alistair and half hoping it would land on anyone else. Finally, it began to wobble and slow. It made its last circuit around the group before landing . . . on Monica.

"*Seriously*?!" she howled as everyone around the circle laughed. "Come on, that doesn't count. We're both gay." A chorus of voices insisted that the rules were the rules, and you had to kiss whoever it landed on. Alvin grinned. Of all the people he might have been paired with, Monica was the least stressful. He wasn't into her. She wasn't into him. There would be no expectation of him doing much, and no gossip later about what it meant. Finally, still grumbling, Monica moved forward. She grabbed Alvin by the back of his head and pulled him forward for a quick peck. It was more of a collision than a kiss and earned them some boos from the crowd. But those turned to laughter as Monica pretended to swoon, shouting, "I'm cured!"

After that, the pressure mostly disappeared and Alvin started to enjoy himself. After her turn, Monica came back to sit next to him. She leaned her head on his shoulder and provided a running commentary on the messy breakups and other drama between various players. When Robyn's spin landed on the girl Alistair had been talking to before, Monica only said her name was Joey. Then she fell curiously silent, which Alvin took to mean there was some kind of history there. The kiss between Joey and Robyn went on longer than most, as they ignored the jeers and catcalls from around the circle. When Joey's turn matched her with Alvin, he assumed it was another lucky pairing with someone there'd be no mutual interest with. As they both crawled forward to meet in the centre of the circle, she towered over him, even though they were kneeling. She seemed even more nervous about the game than Alvin had been. He felt he should say something reassuring, but couldn't think of anything that wouldn't embarrass her, or him, or both of them. Tucking her hair behind her ears, Joey bent down and gave Alvin a surprisingly passionate kiss. When they separated, he sat back on his heels, looking shocked.

"I'm still, like, totally, *totally* gay, but *wow*," he said, causing her to blush deeply and earning another round of laughter from the circle. As Alvin returned to his spot, he saw Monica's expression had darkened, and that Robyn was trying to signal something to her from across the room. He wasn't sure what exactly was bothering her. Was it that the kiss was more impressive than the one they had shared, or was it who it had been with? An ex-friend? An ex-girlfriend? It was a story no one in the Trio had ever talked about.

Alvin didn't get a chance to investigate, though, as Robyn and Wes abruptly called out, "Let's play something else!" Neither of them offered any suggestions, and the circle broke into a confused argument before Monica stood, swaying unsteadily. "I vote," she slurred, holding up a finger, "Seven minutes in heaven." She walked over to the bottle, using it to gesture as she declared, "Alvin and . . . Alistair!" Wes and Robyn quickly hurried over to support her from either side as she dropped the bottle, and everyone looked around uncertainly. Alistair caught Alvin's eye. Though he looked embarrassed, Alistair shrugged as if to say, "Why not?"

Alvin felt his stomach clench. Then, draining the last of his punch, he nodded. Why not?

14 Heart on My Sleeve

THE BEDROOM THEY ENDED UP IN was fairly plain, compared to the extravagance of the other rooms. Alistair explained that it was his favourite in the entire house. He didn't mention how many of the other bedrooms he'd been in, or why. Alvin was nervous enough about what was going to happen, or supposed to happen, that he wasn't really paying attention. When Alistair sat down on the bed and asked, "So what do you think?" Alvin finally looked up, and then did a double-take.

Every item in the room, from the bedsheets to the lampshade to the clock on the wall, was emblazoned with the Coca Cola logo. The shelves were lined with actual bottles of Coke, presumably from different eras, though Alvin couldn't see much of a difference. There was Coke stationery, Coke wallpaper, what looked like a Coca Cola Santa suit hanging up in the closet. At Alvin's expression, Alistair giggled. "I know, right? It's *amazing*. So weird."

Alvin sat down beside Alistair. He looked around with his mouth hanging open, his anxiety put aside for the moment as he tried to figure out why anyone would have a room like this. Alistair leaned in to explain, "Rich people do weird shit with their money, huh? *My* parents definitely do. I figured this room was weird enough to make this feel, uh, less weird."

Alvin smiled gratefully. But the mention of what they were doing brought his anxiety back full force. The confidence he'd felt during the game, surrounded by other people, was quickly fading now that he was alone with Alistair, Coca Cola bedsheets or not. Alistair slipped his hand into Alvin's and squeezed it gently. They sat like that for a few moments, and Alvin felt a fluttering in his stomach. It was not quite the weight that usually built when he thought of situations like this, but not quite excitement either. He worried that all of the alcohol sloshing around in his stomach would pick this moment to come back up. He wondered if this was what everyone else felt when they were alone together for the first time. He wondered what the "normal" feeling was supposed to be in this situation. That was the hardest part of figuring out who, or what, he was interested in. No one had given him a guide, some way to tell whether what he was feeling was the right thing, the expected thing.

Alistair turned slightly and brought his legs up onto the bed so that he was facing Alvin. He kept his hand in his lap as he looked Alvin in the eye. "Look," he said, "if you're not into this, it's cool. Really. We don't have to do anything."

Alvin shook his head quickly. He silently appreciated the concern, but was worried that if he ran away from this now, he'd never have the confidence to try something like it again. "No, I'm . . . I'm into it. Really. I mean, if you are."

Alistair nodded. He smiled gently as he ran his other hand up Alvin's arm and then down to the small of his back. "Totally. Into it . . . and into you."

They shifted positions slightly as they moved closer, figuring out the angles and intersections that were most comfortable between their two bodies. Alvin was easily a foot shorter than Alistair, so there were a few moments of awkward shifting as they tried to find what worked. Alvin wanted to giggle at the absurdity of trying to match themselves up, but didn't want to ruin the mood. This would be his first kiss, his first *real* kiss. With a boy and not one of the girls during the game, and not the practising he and Melissa had done when they were nine. His mind was filled with competing excitement and anxiety. He felt as if every part of his body was detached from him, a series of unrelated elements that he was trying to help Alistair find a place for. Alvin struggled to focus on the kiss itself, to enjoy it. But it was hard.

Alistair's lips were soft, yielding, not as determined as Alvin would have expected given Alistair's personality. Alvin had thought that kissing Alistair would be like talking to him — fast, decisive, maybe a little forceful. Instead, Alistair lingered, explored. He broke away to brush his lips against the side of Alvin's neck, the edge of his ear, the hollow of his throat. After they'd been kissing a while, Alistair's tongue darted forward into Alvin's mouth. When Alvin couldn't help but recoil slightly, Alistair broke off, searching Alvin's face for approval or disapproval. Alvin faked a smile, hoping that he just appeared shy and inexperienced. But inside he felt a rising panic. Alistair continued with increased enthusiasm. His hands wandered under Alvin's shirt and along his waist. Alvin clumsily followed suit, though he found it harder and harder to pay attention. In his head, he was playing out the next few seconds, the next minute. Would Alistair's attention shift farther down? Would he want to undress? For Alvin to undress? Should Alvin talk? Should he ask to slow down, or would that ruin the mood completely and bring everything to a stop?

As Alistair leaned down to suck gently on Alvin's neck, it became too much for Alvin. It felt good, in a distant way, but the slight pain seemed to break the spell he was under. He pushed away, but misjudged the distance to the edge of the bed and fell to the floor. Alistair leaped up, concerned, and reached out to help Alvin up. Alvin could only hug his knees, tears welling up in his eyes. What was wrong with him? Why was he screwing this up? Why couldn't he just enjoy what was happening, what he was supposed to want to happen? Alistair was asking if he was okay, if they were moving too fast, but Alvin couldn't bring himself to answer.

They were interrupted by a series of knocks and Monica's muffled voice calling Alvin's name from beyond the door. Over the thumping music that filled the house, they could hear Robyn and Wes asking if everything was going all right. All three of them were barely able to contain their giggling. Monica yelled, "Seven minutes is up!" Before either Alistair or Alvin could respond, the door swung open and the Trio spilled into their room, only to stop short when they saw Alvin on the ground and Alistair awkwardly standing over him.

This was exactly what Alvin had been afraid of. This was his worst expectation of coming to the party — that he would try to do everything normally, would mess it up somehow, and everyone would find out that he just wasn't capable of being normal. His eyes darted between Alistair and Monica and Robyn and Wes, seeing their surprise, their confused concern. He had no idea what to say to reassure them. Alvin had never felt very good at explaining what he was feeling, and now he was too drunk, too overwhelmed, too emotional to even try. Instead, he shouldered his way past them. He ran down the stairs out of the house, and into the night.

15 In the Lonely Hour

RIGHT AWAY, ALVIN REGRETTED running out into the frigid December night. He'd been wearing his boots already, but he hadn't stopped to retrieve his jacket from the pile in one of the many bedrooms. So he stumbled along, hugging himself to keep warm. He cursed the long and winding driveway he had to follow before he got anywhere near the road. At least there was no snow — score one for climate change.

Behind him, Alvin heard the front door slam and

the voices of the Trio calling his name. A part of him was touched that they had come after him. But he was still processing, and trying to reassure them would be too much for him to manage right now. He'd rather take his chances with the cold.

Alvin walked as quickly as he could along the dimly lit stretch of road, worried that one of Jesse's rich neighbours would come tearing past. Death by luxury SUV was not the way Alvin wanted to go. Neither was hypothermia. He hoped that the bus shelter would provide some warmth, or at least that the next bus would come before he froze to death. He was rapidly sobering up, from the cold and from obsessing over what had happened back at the party. *Alistair must hate me*, he thought. *The Trio must hate me. Everyone at the party, at school, in the whole world must hate me.*

Halfway to the stop, Alvin saw someone approaching from the opposite direction. A figure that was better dressed for the cold than Alvin, and lit by the red glow of a cigarette — Rowan.

As Alvin approached, Rowan dropped the cigarette and ground it out with his heel. He held his hands up in an exaggerated gesture of surrender. "You caught me. Late to the party, *and* smoking. What would Dougherty say?"

Alvin grinned, unable to match Rowan's chuckle and glad that the darkness obscured the tears slowly freezing on his cheeks. Rowan took one look at Alvin stamping and hugging himself and pulled off his trademark denim jacket. He held it out until Alvin stopped protesting and put it on.

"Come on, Alvin, you must be freezing. Let's get to Jesse's." Alvin's expression must have darkened, because Rowan changed tack and suggested, "Or let's go to the bus shelter. That's probably closer, right?"

When they reached the shelter, Alvin took off Rowan's jacket and tried to return it, and it was Rowan's turn to protest. Finally, they compromised and huddled together on the bench with it draped it over both their shoulders. Alvin doubted the jacket was doing much to warm them that way. But being close to each other helped, and definitely helped distract Alvin from worrying about the cold. He was nervous about being alone with Rowan, after how badly things had gone with Alistair. But he was grateful for it as well. He could try again, with no witnesses or judgment.

As if sensing his thoughts, Rowan said, "No pressure, like none at all. But if you want to talk about why you left the party, we can."

Alvin tensed up, but then he thought about it. What could it hurt?

"I ended up upstairs. With Alistair. We'd both had a few drinks . . . We kissed. It was nice." Alvin felt the tips of his ears burn as he talked about the encounter. He realized too late that it probably wasn't great to tell his crush about his other crush. Oh well.

Rowan showed no sign of being jealous or angry, though. He turned to look at Alvin carefully. "Did he . . . do something? That you weren't into?"

Alvin shook his head. "No, no, nothing like that. Totally consensual. We were both into it . . . or, I mean. I *was* into it. I said I was into it. Alistair didn't do anything wrong."

Rowan frowned. "You know, consent isn't just

saying yes to whatever the person wants. It's okay to stop things."

Alvin wasn't sure what to say to that. He didn't think Alistair had done anything wrong. Alvin just figured that he'd given Alistair the wrong signals. But the way Rowan phrased it . . . Agreeing to what other people wanted was a pretty accurate summary of Alvin's romantic life since he'd started having one. No one seemed to ask what *he* wanted, or what he was feeling. They made assumptions, or they asked questions Alvin felt awkward saying no to, and only really asked when things were halfway done.

Alvin took a deep breath and let it out shakily. He felt as if he was on the verge of tears again. The last thing he wanted was to cry in the middle of what he was going to try to explain.

"I'm gay," Alvin started.

This prompted a chuckle from Rowan, who apologized and gestured for him to continue.

Alvin gave him a quick smile. That fact, at least, was no longer in question. "I'm gay. I know I'm gay. I know I like guys, and that I want a boyfriend. And a cute little apartment in Toronto with a dog that he and I spoil."

This time, he and Rowan laughed together at such a cliché.

Alvin's expression turned serious again. "But . . . sex? I don't know if I want that. I mean I'm fine with some stuff, I *like* some stuff. But when things get too intense . . . or even just talking about things getting intense, I . . ." Alvin trailed off, unable to put into words the weight that built in his stomach, the panic that burst forth. He always felt he was being pulled out to sea by the riptide of what everyone else expected. Drowning in the endless ocean of what he *should* enjoy, what he *should* want to do. With his body, and with other people's bodies. He closed his eyes. He braced himself for Rowan's response and dreaded it, already regretting his decision to explain.

"You shut down," Rowan offered.

Alvin looked up, nodding, surprised to be so clearly understood.

Rowan reached over. He waited for Alvin to nod again before he took his hand. "Look, that happens. We go through shit. Whether it's obvious to everybody around us, or something we don't even realize until it's over. And either way, it spills over into how we feel about everything else. But we get to decide what we want to do about it."

Alvin knew he looked skeptical.

Rowan laughed. "Okay, okay, I maybe stole that from my therapist. I'm not an expert at figuring this stuff out. I just mean, if you want to date someone and never go past kissing, you can do that. You shouldn't have to do anything beyond that just because it seems like the right thing to do. If they're expecting that, they're not the right person. And the right person exists." Rowan stared at Alvin for a long moment, and then looked away and shrugged. "I don't know if that made any kind of sense." He seemed frustrated that he couldn't clearly explain his point.

Alvin briefly enjoyed being on the other side of that frustration for once. Then he squeezed Rowan's hand and said softly, "I get what you mean. Thank you."

They sat together in silence, watching the occasional car make its lonely way down the road and break up the darkness with the sweeping glare of headlights. Alvin wasn't sure where he would even take the bus when it arrived. The plan had been to crash at Jesse's with the Trio. Melissa's house would take hours to get to this late at night. Going home would tip off his parents that something had happened, and he was too tired and emotional to deal with their questions.

Rowan tapped Alvin gently on the arm to bring him back from his thoughts. "If you still want to leave, that's cool," he said, watching as the bus slowly wheezed its way toward them. "But we *could* just head back to the party. Together."

The bus doors thumped open and spilled light out onto the street. Alvin waved it away. He turned back to Rowan and grinned. "Why not? I bet everyone's too drunk now to even remember me leaving."

Rowan grinned back. He stood and arranged his jacket across both of their shoulders again. "Exactly. And if that doesn't work, we'll drink until *we* don't remember."

Laughing, they made their way back up the road to the mansion.

16 Closer to Fine

AS ALVIN HAD THOUGHT, the party had continued to rage on in his absence. No one seemed to have taken note of his disastrous encounter with Alistair. He stood awkwardly in the foyer, not sure what he would say to Alistair when he ran into him again. Or to the Trio, for that matter. When he was talking to Rowan, his reaction had seemed sensible, understandable. But when Alvin tried to summon up the words to explain, they swam just out of his reach.

Rowan looped his arm through Alvin's and started to pull him deeper into the house. When Alvin resisted, Rowan withdrew, looking confused. "I thought we'd head to the kitchen. Get some drinks?"

Alvin nodded, trying his best to smile. But all he could think of was being confronted by Alistair at any moment. "Yeah, that sounds great, I just . . . I want to apologize to the Trio. And to Alistair. Before they see me . . ."

Alvin didn't finish the sentence, but what he was worried about was obvious to both of them. He wanted to talk to Alistair and the Trio before they saw him hanging out with another cute boy, after he had run out of the house to get away from one. Rowan nodded and returned the smile. But Alvin saw a flash of hurt on his face and his heart sank. He wanted to explain to Rowan that it wasn't a rejection, just a delay. But he wasn't sure how to word it without making it sound like there was something between them. Alvin felt that there was, but maybe he was too hopeful. If Rowan was just being understanding, the last thing Alvin needed was to ruin that by interpreting it as romantic interest.

"Sure, yeah," Rowan said. "Of course. You find them, and I'll grab us drinks. We can meet back in the living room."

Alvin made a face, and Rowan chuckled. "The living room with the stuffed alligator. Third room on the right from the kitchen? I'll wait for you there."

Alvin nodded gratefully, then set off to make his apologies. He hoped that he would figure out what to say by the time he had to say it. He wandered through every room on the first floor that wasn't off limits. Then he went upstairs, thinking that Alistair might still be in the Coca Cola bedroom — hopefully not with someone else. Finding it empty, Alvin doubled back, only to run into Jesse. He was emerging from what Alvin figured was his bedroom with a vape pen dangling from his hand.

"Oh, hey, Alvin!" Jesse said. "I thought you left. Want to come for a swim?" Jesse had changed into a speedo that left little to the imagination. His body was lean and toned, and Alvin was suddenly very aware of how private the hallway felt.

Alvin stammered and blushed. Jesse laughed and stretched out his arm to lean against the wall Alvin was backed up against. He jerked his head toward the open bedroom door. Beyond, Alvin could see a massive bed with satiny sheets.

Taking another drag from the pen, Jesse let out a puff of vapour. He tilted his head to try to catch Alvin's eyes. "Or . . . we could just hang out up here. I've got plenty of this to share." He waved the vape pen between them, raising his eyebrows suggestively.

Alvin gave a nervous laugh and ducked under Jesse's arm to head back toward the stairs. "Um, y'know what, I'm good," he said. "Don't let me keep you from swimming. I was actually just seeing if Alistair was still up here."

At the mention of Alistair, Jesse's face fell, and Alvin felt a little bad for him. The look of surprise and rejection on his face was painfully clear, though it was quickly replaced by Jesse's usual placid grin. Jesse shrugged, right back to his easygoing self. Alvin suspected it was his go-to strategy for dealing with an uncomfortable situation.

"Oh yeah, for sure," drawled Jesse. "No worries. I think Alistair and the Trio headed down to the basement. I'll, uh, catch you later."

Jesse's basement was as lavish as the rest of the house, with a huge part of it set up like a private movie theatre. Next to that was yet another bedroom. There was a home office, the door of which was covered in the Halloween-style *Caution* tape that Jesse had used to mark rooms as off-limits. Finally Alvin came to a lounge with a pool table. He could hear the voices of the Trio and saw Alistair lining up his shot. But as soon as he stepped into sight, the conversation ceased. He assumed it was because they'd been talking about him.

Alvin gave a sheepish wave, still working out how to start his apology. Before he could say anything, the Trio gave one another a look and announced they were heading outside to smoke a joint. It was a flimsy excuse, given the liberty with which everyone else at the party was smoking in the house. But Alvin was grateful for the chance to talk to Alistair first, to try to explain without having to provide others with a play-by-play of what had happened. Alistair laid down his pool cue and hopped up to sit on the edge of the table. He gestured for Alvin to join him. Alvin's hop up took a few tries and was much less graceful — Alistair had a foot or so of height on Alvin and the table wasn't exactly low to the ground. They both laughed, and the tension that had been building since Alvin came back eased.

"I'm sorry if I did anything you weren't ready for," Alistair began.

Alvin shook his head and held up his hand to stop him from saying anything more. "No, you were fine . . . I mean, yes, it felt a little too fast. But I should have talked to you more. Before we did anything. It wasn't fair for me to just run out."

They sat together quietly for a few moments. Alvin nervously spun one of the pool balls as he tried to find the right words to explain. Alistair waited patiently for him to continue.

Finally, Alvin said, "It's like everyone has an idea of what they're ready for, right? And they follow that idea, and it's fine. But I . . . I'm still figuring out what that idea even *is* for me. I'm still at that step."

Alistair thought over Alvin's words, nodding. Then he laid his hand on Alvin's. "Can I ask you some things, then? Honest answers?"

"Of course."

"Do you like me?"

Alvin looked away, blushing. He couldn't help but smile at Alistair's innocent, genuine tone. He looked back, and nodded. "Yes. Yeah, I do."

Alistair smiled back. "Okay, then we just have to figure out where we start, and take it from there. Holding hands — how was that?"

"Nice. That was really nice."

"Kissing?"

"That too."

"Tongue?"

Alvin looked away again. He gave a nervous laugh.

Alistair hopped down. He moved to stand in front

of Alvin and took both of his hands. For once, they were almost the same height. "Seriously, Alvin. I want to know. And if it wasn't okay, I want to know that too."

"It was . . ." Alvin thought back to the Coke room, what seemed like hours ago. "It was a little surprising. But I liked it. I think. Would try it again."

They giggled together, and Alistair nodded, looking excited. "Okay, okay, that's good! French kissing. We can start with that. What is that? Like, first and a half base?"

Alvin frowned thoughtfully and shrugged. "I dunno. I never really understood the whole baseball metaphor. My parents are more into cricket."

"That doesn't use bases?"

"Nah, I think they use, like . . . a bunch of little sticks. Stumps. Something like that."

They laughed again and, after a moment, Alistair leaned in to kiss Alvin. It was more hesitant than before, and Alistair kept his eyes open to watch Alvin's reaction. But that was fine. Instead of the weight building in his stomach, Alvin felt butterflies.

17 People Like Us

"YOU'RE SURE YOU CAN'T STAY?" Alvin stared up at Alistair. He hoped his expression wasn't as desperate as the question sounded.

They had kissed, and talked, and kissed some more. But Alistair had confessed that he couldn't stay for midnight. His parents were sending a car to bring him to whatever fundraiser or mixer or gala event they were at. Alvin teased him gently about having better places to be, but he could see that Alistair really did want to stay.

As Alvin waved goodbye and turned to head back into the house, the glow of their make-out session started to fade. He thought guiltily about how he had essentially abandoned Rowan after promising they'd brave the party together. He had intended to find him again. But he had also been expecting Alistair to want nothing to do with him. As he reached the front door, Alvin looked up from his thoughts to see Rowan pulling on his coat to leave.

"Oh, hey," Alvin said. "I . . . I was just about to look for you."

Rowan smirked and looked pointedly over Alvin's shoulder at the retreating headlights of Alistair's cab. Alvin flushed and started to stammer an apology, but Rowan cut him off. "Don't worry about it. I'm glad things worked out with him."

Rowan shouldered his way past Alvin. Then he paused and turned back, his expression softening. "Really. I'm glad you worked things out. And if you want to talk through stuff, we can talk."

Alvin nodded gratefully. After a moment's

hesitation, he stepped forward to give Rowan a quick hug. They embraced for a few seconds. Alvin's nose was pressed into Rowan's denim-clad shoulder, inhaling the rich scent of clove cigarettes. He felt the same butterflies in his stomach as he'd felt with Alistair. As they separated, it was clear Rowan was feeling as conflicted as Alvin over the way the evening had gone. Alvin felt the pang of guilt return.

Rowan started making his way up the long and winding driveway. Just before he rounded the curve and moved out of sight, Rowan turned back. He spoke through cupped hands so his voice would carry. "You should try Glad Day again — maybe on your own this time. You know, if you want to get advice from someone who *isn't* already into you." He turned back around and disappeared into the dark.

At that distance, there was no way Rowan could have seen the look on Alvin's face, or the way the tips of his ears were burning red. But Alvin suspected he knew exactly what kind of reaction that admission would cause. And Alvin didn't really mind.

Alvin woke early New Year's Day. It was much later than he would have woken up at home, but still long before anyone else in Jesse's house. He lay awake for a while, marvelling at how still everything seemed compared to the night before. As he got up and quietly dressed, the Trio barely stirred. Rowan had given Alvin an idea, a New Year's Resolution. After double-checking that he could still get home before his parents got suspicious, he collected his things and headed downtown.

Hardly anyone was around, on the subway or in the streets, and most of the businesses that Alvin passed were closed. Glad Day was the exception. He knew they prided themselves on being open every day of the year, no matter what, for whoever might need to go somewhere quiet and calm. The only other person in the store was stocking shelves. As they turned to greet him, Alvin felt a flash of embarrassment as he recognized Bree, the clerk who had chased out him and the Trio.

Bree recognized him as well, raising their eyebrows and glancing in the direction of the erotica shelf. "Just you this time? You know, this is the one day I *wouldn't* kick out your friends for getting loud."

Alvin started to apologize, but Bree waved him to silence with an amused expression. "I'm just giving you a hard time, kid. Perks of the job. What are you looking for?"

Alvin had set out with the intention of finding something to teach him how to date or get comfortable around Alistair. Or even a how-to guide about gay sex. *Something* to help him be less awkward. Maybe, hopefully, to help him enjoy the stuff the Trio talked about instead of feeling nauseous and overwhelmed when it was mentioned. But he found himself thinking of none of those things. Instead, he remembered the paper birds and the different flags they represented.

"Do you . . ." Alvin started, suddenly feeling self-conscious. At Bree's encouraging smile, he tried again, the words coming out in a rush. "Do you have any books about hating sex?"

Alvin clapped a hand to his mouth, mortified. He had never said it out loud, not in those words. With Alistair and Rowan, with the Trio, even with Melissa, he'd always phrased it as not being ready. But as he said what he said, it felt true.

Bree reacted as if Alvin had said he was looking for a book with a blue cover. They nodded thoughtfully, shelving the book they were holding. Then they beckoned for Alvin to follow them through the nonfiction section. "Can I ask some follow-up questions?"

Alvin nodded, his stomach already sinking at the thought of being grilled about what was wrong with him.

"Have you had sex before?"

"No! I mean, no. I haven't."

"Have you *wanted* to have sex before?"

"Uh . . . no. Not really."

"Have you dated anyone? Or had a crush even?"

Alvin thought about Alistair, and Rowan, and even Jesse. He had felt something around each of them. An excitement, a nervousness, a curiosity to learn more about the side of them that no one else saw. If that wasn't a crush, what was?

"Yeah," he replied. Then he hurriedly added, "Not dated, I mean. Just . . . um . . . wanted to date? I think. But not, like, other stuff. Just to know them, I guess. I don't know if that counts."

Bree laughed. Seeing Alvin's stricken expression, they held up their hands. "Sorry, sorry, really, I didn't mean to laugh. It absolutely counts. You just described *my* whole love life. So, yeah, it counts." They tapped one of the patches on their vest. It looked like a playing card spade striped with grey and purple.

Alvin smiled nervously. He was surprised that Bree was taking him seriously, had actually asked how he felt about sex and dating. But he couldn't quite believe that anyone else had the same problems he did. Especially not someone who was out of high school, was working in the Village, and seemed to have life figured out.

Bree pulled a book off the shelf. "This is *The Invisible Orientation*, probably the best thing to start with if you're still figuring stuff out."

Alvin nodded in agreement — basic introduction was definitely where he was at. At the cash, Alvin pulled out his wallet, but Bree waved a hand dismissively. "Listen, you can come back and buy all the other books you want, whenever you want. This one's on me." They took a business card from a stack by the register, scribbled something on the back, then held it out for Alvin to take. Their tone became gentle. "Being a teenager is hard enough to figure out. Being queer makes it harder. And being ace? It's a lot. I didn't have any books — or bookstore managers — when I was your age. Let me pay it forward."

Alvin took the card, overcome with gratitude. He didn't trust himself to say anything, so he focused his attention on what he was holding — the number for something called the LGBT Youth Line and Bree's personal store email. As Alvin tucked it carefully into the first few pages of the book, Bree nodded and said, "You have questions about being ace, or gay, or anything really . . . call them. Or text. They're there to answer questions. And if you're not ready to do that yet — if you don't feel you can ask a stranger — then write me instead. I might not reply right away, but I'll reply. Okay?"

Alvin wanted to hug them, but knew that would be inappropriate. Bree didn't look like the free hugs type, anyway. Instead, Alvin just nodded, tears in his eyes. He clutched the book to his chest as he stepped out into the street, ready to face the new year.

18 Constant Craving

"OKAY, WHICH ONE DO YOU WANT to take care of this time? Snacks or tickets?" asked Alistair.

Alvin furrowed his brow as if in deep thought. He tapped a finger against his lips as he looked at the equally long lines on opposite sides of the cinema. This was his fourth date with Alistair, and their fourth date at the movies. Alvin knew Tuesday evenings were the only free spot in Alistair's schedule. When he'd asked Alvin out after the winter break, Alistair had brought his agenda so he could pen Alvin in.

"Y'know, I could pay for both, if you —"

Alvin quickly shook his head. He stood on tiptoes to kiss Alistair's cheek before heading for the concession counter. He appreciated Alistair's offer to pay — Alistair *always* offered to pay. But it made Alvin uneasy, as if Alistair thought he couldn't afford to go to the movies. True, Alvin blew through more money on their weekly movie dates than he normally spent in a month. But if that was the cost of finally being in a relationship, he was willing to pay it.

Once he and Alistair had chosen their seats, Alvin tried to quiet the anxiety that normally blossomed in the dark. They put the drink between them and passed the popcorn back and forth, as usual. Alistair took Alvin's hand in his, as usual. And when he got bored with the story, Alvin knew Alistair would put his arm around him and move in for a kiss — as usual. Alvin didn't mind kissing when they had a moment alone. But every date followed the same script, one where the theatre was just a place for them to make out. When it was a movie Alvin didn't care much about, it annoyed him a bit. But when it was one he actually wanted to watch — he *loved* romantic comedies — he found it too irritating to ignore. It felt like a silly thing to bring up, especially when every other teenage couple around them was busy making out as well. So Alvin hadn't said anything.

They held hands through the first act, as boy met girl and both pretended they wanted nothing to do with each other. Alvin wanted to make a joke about straight couples, like he would with the Trio or even Melissa. But he knew that Alistair was one of those people who hated to talk during movies. Even movies he wasn't interested in. Alvin couldn't help but sneak glances at Alistair's face every few minutes. He could see Alistair's attention starting to wane, though Alistair gave him a reassuring smile every time he caught Alvin looking. At least Alistair was *trying* to enjoy the movie, since he knew Alvin wanted to see it.

Alvin slipped his hand out of Alistair's grasp to take a sip from their drink. At least his palms didn't get as sweaty now as the first time they'd met. Then disaster struck. Freed from hand-holding, Alistair's hand casually reached down to Alvin's knee and gave his leg an affectionate squeeze. It wasn't much further than they'd gone at Jesse's party, but Alistair's fingers grazing the inside of his thigh made Alvin's anxiety spike. He jerked up in his seat, spilling soda on himself. He swore loudly enough that people turned to glare at him. Alistair blinked in surprise and pulled his hand back. Alvin tried to mime that he was fine before muttering, "bathroom," and shuffling away as fast as the other guests in their row would let him.

Outside the theatre, Alvin leaned against the wall. He closed his eyes and let out a deep breath. Then he pulled out his phone and dialed Melissa's number as he walked to the bathroom to clean off.

"*Please* tell me you're not calling me during your date. Again," Melissa said.

"Okay, that time it was because . . . You know what? It doesn't matter. I don't think I can do this."

"Do what, Alvin? See a movie? You've been doing that fine!"

"No, do . . . *this*, this whole dating thing, being alone with him. I just . . ." Alvin sighed. He awkwardly pinned the phone to his ear with his shoulder as he dabbed at the stain on his shirt with paper towel. "I feel like he's just waiting for us to get to the good stuff. He doesn't even like movies!"

"Well, that's ridiculous. Everyone likes movies."

"He said he prefers *documentaries*."

"Okay, *I* wouldn't date him. But you're not dating him because of the movies, are you?"

Alvin frowned at his reflection in the mirror. He thought of the reasons he liked Alistair. He was cute. He was smart. He genuinely cared how people were doing and how he could make things better. But what did they really have in common?

"He doesn't have to be, like, *the one*, you know," Melissa continued. She was used to Alvin's pained silences. "He just has to be the one you want to spend time with, for now. And you do, right?"

"I guess," Alvin said reluctantly. "I just don't know why he'd want to spend time with me. Especially if we're not doing . . . anything else."

"So what if you're just kissing and holding hands? You said he got where you were at with that stuff."

"He did . . . he does. I mean, I think he does. I just feel like he's waiting for more. Like he's waiting for me to be worth dating." Alvin could picture Melissa's expression as she prepared to hype him up about how he was already worthwhile. So he quickly continued. "I know, I know. I'm already worth dating. I'm wonderful. I'm perfect."

"Whoa, whoa, whoa. I would never say you're *perfect*."

Alvin chuckled, then sighed again. "I guess I mean it doesn't feel like there's anything there, if we're not making out. So if we don't go further than that . . ."

"Look, Alvin, you know my policy with guys. Even when there's sex . . . maybe especially when there is sex, if you don't feel like you're getting anything, then you have to talk about it, or . . ."

"Or what? Break up? I only started dating him a month ago!"

Alvin elbowed the door open and stepped out, only to stop dead. Melissa's voice grew distant as he let the phone fall away from his ear.

Alistair stood just outside the bathroom. His expression of patient concern rapidly became one of embarrassment. "Break up?" Alistair asked, his voice wavering. Alvin couldn't tell if he was sad or angry.

"No, I didn't mean . . . I was just telling Melissa about how you . . . how we . . ."

Alistair turned abruptly, dumped their popcorn and drink in the garbage, and walked quickly toward the exit.

Alvin ended the call and shoved his phone in his pocket. He jogged to keep pace with Alistair's much longer stride. "Look, I'm sorry. I was just freaking out."

Alistair stayed silent until they were in the parking lot. Then he rounded on Alvin so suddenly, Alvin almost ran into him. "If you're freaking out, then you should *talk* to me! You said you'd be honest."

Alvin started to apologize, and then stopped, his

own anger rising. "I did . . . I mean, I have been. But we don't really talk, we just sit together. And make out. And watch movies you don't even want to see. When would we have talked about it?"

Alistair's eyes flashed, and he looked like he was about to yell. Then he brought his hands up to massage his temples, taking a deep breath in and exhaling shakily. "Okay. You're right. We haven't really had a lot of time, and going to the movies isn't great for conversations. But if something's wrong, I want you to tell me."

Alvin nodded. He tried to find the words to describe how he'd been feeling. Before he could, Alistair continued. "I mean, I'm happy to go as slow as you want, to wait as long as you need to. I don't want to rush you."

"See, but that's the problem. It's not about just going slow, it's . . . like, what if I never want to do that other stuff? What if kissing and hand-holding is as far as I want to go?"

For once, Alistair was at a loss for words.

19 Sorrows and Glories

THE CAR RIDE BACK to Alvin's house was incredibly awkward. But the breakup was more or less friendly. It wasn't until a few weeks later at school that Alvin started to hear the whispers in the hall and the caf about what had happened and why.

"I heard Alistair dumped him cause he wouldn't put out."

"I heard it was a pity date, and Alvin was *totally* ungrateful."

"Alistair's, like, *totally* a catch. Alvin was *way* out of his league."

It was frustrating, but nobody ever came to Alvin for any details. And while Alistair didn't seem to be the source of the rumours, he certainly wasn't doing anything to stop the talk. He was only concerned with people knowing he hadn't done anything wrong. As a result, everyone jumped to the conclusion that Alvin must have done something wrong instead. The Trio was sympathetic, but were trying to be neutral. They were friends with both Alistair and Alvin, and they hoped that everything would smooth over soon. The green room became as uncomfortable for Alvin as after their trip to the Village. Alistair was never there for very long, but he was always *around*. Alvin didn't know how to talk to him with all the gossip.

Instead, Alvin found himself having lunch on the bleachers again, watching Jesse and the other jocks trying to play soccer on the slippery, frozen field. The first Tuesday of February, Alvin trudged out to his usual spot only to find Rowan already there, discreetly smoking a cigarette out of view of the main building.

"Oh, uh . . . hey," Alvin greeted him. "I thought your lunch was next period."

Rowan sat up in surprise, about to flick the cigarette away. He relaxed when he realized it was Alvin. "Oh, yeah. I had to change to a different bio class so I can leave early. Dougherty's *pissed*. But there's not much she can do about it when I have a doctor's note."

Rowan held out the cigarette to Alvin, who waved it away.

"Where do you *go*, anyways?" Alvin put a hand to his mouth. That had come out a lot more bluntly than he had meant it to. But the last couple of weeks had really cut into his patience.

Luckily, Rowan laughed, amused by Alvin's uncharacteristic boldness. He shook his head as Alvin started to apologize. "No, no, it's cool. Everyone thinks I skip class for fun, or that I have some mystery illness. When I transferred here last year, there was a rumour I was dealing drugs at other schools." Rowan gestured toward the field with his cigarette. "I think I can thank Jesse for that one." He took another drag, looking sideways at Alvin. "The truth is . . . shit, I don't think anyone ever just asked me before. But, yeah, anyways. There's no doctor in Mississauga that specializes in transitioning, so I have to go to the city. Right near Glad Day. That's why I hang out there all the time."

Alvin nodded. Then, leaning into his newfound bluntness, he said, "That's pretty shitty. Having to travel all that way."

Rowan laughed and nodded. "You're not wrong! But that's how it is. I'm used to it."

Alvin sat thoughtfully for a few moments. Then he asked, cautiously, "How come your parents don't drive you in?"

Rowan didn't answer right away, and Alvin worried he'd pressed too far. Finally, Rowan stubbed out the cigarette. He swung around so that he was facing the field beside Alvin, their knees brushing. "My parents don't really know about it. I haven't talked to them since I moved here." At Alvin's look of confusion,

Rowan explained, "When I came out, they weren't exactly supportive. Small town, shitty thinking. So, I moved in with my Aunt Liv. She's pretty chill. She's a librarian slash beekeeper slash all-around badass. She doesn't always get me, but she supports me."

They sat for a few minutes in silence. Then Rowan leaned over and bumped Alvin playfully with his shoulder. "Okay, that was enough of a downer. Tell me what's up with you."

Alvin groaned, putting his hands over his eyes. "Ugh. Definitely not less of a downer."

"I mean, I heard about you and Alistair."

"Yeah, that's part of the problem. Everyone's heard."

Rowan shrugged. "It'll pass. Everyone likes to talk about stuff they don't know anything about, until the next thing happens."

Alvin went silent again, brooding.

Rowan bumped him again. "Hey. Tell me about it."

Alvin took a deep breath and plunged into it. He

talked about the hopefulness he'd felt after talking with Alistair the second time on New Year's. The frustration and uncertainty he'd felt when they'd actually started to date. The feeling he wasn't good enough, or just wasn't enough.

Rowan listened to it all patiently, and thoughtfully. He waited until Alvin was done to offer his opinion. "I think that was really brave of you. To admit that it wasn't working. I don't know that I would have done that."

Alvin was shocked. He couldn't imagine a situation Rowan wouldn't respond to with casual calm. It couldn't be that Alvin was the brave one out of the two of them. Shyly, he mimicked Rowan, leaning over to bump him with his shoulder. "You helped me with that, you know. Talking me through it. Just like now."

Rowan shrugged. He looked embarrassed by Alvin's attempt at praise. "I remember not having anyone to talk to, when I was going through it — before I even knew what I was going through. I made a lot of bad choices, before and after I started transitioning.

Hooking up with Jesse was one of those." They both snickered, and Rowan turned slightly to look Alvin in the eye as he continued. "I realized, after all that, that sex didn't make me feel any closer to who I was. I had to figure that shit out for myself. Not from anyone's approval, or their interest. Does that make sense?"

Alvin nodded. They sat for a while longer, huddled together against the February chill. They didn't talk about much else, but for Alvin, that was fine. They didn't need to.

20 Tempest On A Teacup

AS SOON AS IT WAS CLEAR that Alvin was spending time with Rowan, the rumours increased. People assumed that Rowan was a rebound. Some even suggested Alvin had cheated on Alistair with him, and that's what had prompted the breakup.

Alvin couldn't deny that his crush on Rowan remained alive and well. But the deepening of their friendship was exactly that — nothing romantic or unrequited. Sometimes Alvin daydreamed that it might become something more, but he was committed to staying single at least until he understood himself a bit better.

Reading *The Invisible Orientation* helped, but Alvin had always done better talking about something rather than reading about it. He and Rowan would go over the nuances of queer sexuality over burgers, or riding the bus, giggling with each other when people nearby gave them strange looks. It took a while, but finally Alvin learned the terms that fit best with what he was feeling. Being into the emotional parts of dating boys but not the physical likely meant he was asexual, but homoromantic. The words felt silly when he first started using them. They felt made up somehow, compared to something as simple and emphatic as saying he was *gay*. But Rowan was quick to remind him that it was just because he wasn't comfortable using them yet. Besides, Rowan pointed out, *all* words were made up.

Alvin emailed Bree at the beginning of March Break, to thank them again for the book and to assure them that he was (finally) reading it. Bree's reply was brief: *"GOOD!"* above an invite to a panel Glad Day was hosting on queer community. Alvin thought of inviting the Trio, but he doubted something like that would hold their interest for very long. Instead, he forwarded the email to Rowan and Melissa. They would both appreciate hearing activists talking about the community. Plus, Alvin thought it was time Melissa and Rowan finally met, since he talked about each of them to the other constantly.

The bookshelves in Glad Day had all been pushed to the sides. The open space left in the middle was filled with a scattering of folding chairs. Bree had waved them in before rushing off to continue preparing for the event. Near the back — just in front of the erotica shelf, Alvin noted with a smirk — sat a few older members of the community. It was a more diverse group than Alvin had expected from what he'd seen when he first came to the Village with the Trio. The crowd, too, showed a range of ages and races and genders. Alvin wasn't sure he'd ever seen a queer person of colour over the age of fifty before.

He couldn't stop wondering where they all went when events like this were over. Where would *he* live when he was that age, and the city was even more expensive?

For the most part, the night was about history and the past. The panelists talked about organizers they'd known and businesses that had closed. How they'd struggled for safety, for the right to live and love openly. Gradually, the conversation turned to Pride as it was now. The corporate sponsorship, the intense partying. The conflicts and chaos as the community split and reunited and split again over issues that were never fully addressed. Alvin felt strangely guilty, wondering what Melissa's opinion on all of this was. He had brought her with the idea of showing her his wonderful and diverse queer community. But now he felt like she was only seeing the negatives. Luckily, Rowan was quick to lean in and provide explanation or context whenever a topic went over their heads, and gradually Alvin relaxed.

The discussion among the panelists came to a close and Bree opened up the talk to questions from the audience. Alvin thought about what he might ask. He had a million questions, but none that he wanted to voice at something this public. While Alvin was trying to decide, a middle-aged man near the front raised his hand. He waited, somewhat impatiently, for the mic to make its way to him. Alvin looked him over and then rolled his eyes at Melissa. Cis-looking, white, expensive haircut and clothes. This was exactly the kind of person Alvin had been afraid the panel would be full of. He could tell this man's view of the community wasn't broad enough to include someone like him. Or like Rowan.

"Hi, I'm Daniel Hollahan, and I've lived here for almost thirty years. Now, my question is more of a comment." The man's words drew a few groans from the audience. "We talk a lot about how Pride has changed. One of the things I can't *stand* is that there's so many people who don't belong there, there's hardly room for gays and lesbians." The groans gave way to grumbling, then outright opposition as he continued. "You know what I mean! Straight couples are —"

Bree quickly jumped in. The mic made their voice boom across the store. "Now, hold on. You can't tell who's straight and who's not. They could be bi, or trans, or —"

Daniel sneered in reply. "If they *look* straight, they shouldn't be at Pride. It's just as bad as saying asexuals belong there. These are just dishonest people who take up resources that *real* gays and lesbians are in need of!"

The crowd began to break into knots of argument. Most people were disagreeing with what he was saying, but more than a few took Daniel's side. Rowan and Melissa immediately bristled, rising out of their seats to join the argument. But to everyone's surprise, including Alvin's, Alvin was the one who stood up first. There was a pause as people looked to Bree, as the moderator. They gestured for Daniel to pass the microphone. Reluctantly, he did. As it went from hand to hand toward where Alvin and his friends were, he almost lost his nerve. Before he could reconsider, though, the mic was in his hand, and people had quieted down to listen. All eyes were on him.

"Hi, um . . . I'm Alvin. I, uh . . . just started coming to Glad Day, and, uh . . ." He faltered, feeling like he was losing the attention of the crowd and finding it hard to match Daniel's impatient glare. Alvin glanced down at Rowan and Melissa, then up at Bree. He thought about how many hours and days and years he'd already been quiet before he met them. He cleared his throat and started again. This time his voice was more confident.

"I'm gay. I've known I was gay since I was a kid. But there were a lot of other things I didn't understand about myself. And it's only from coming here and from talking to other people, people in the community, who are here tonight . . . well, that's the only way that I found out what asexuality was, as a label. And it's a label that fits me, just the same as gay does."

Alvin could feel tears welling up as he spoke, but he let the momentum of what he was saying carry him forward before he lost his nerve.

"I belong here. And I belong at Pride. Whether I'm there with a boyfriend, or there with my best friend." He gestured to Rowan and Melissa as he spoke. He saw they were both still fiercely staring down Daniel on Alvin's behalf. "Whether I know what to call myself, or I'm still figuring it out. Or if I'm only just realizing what there is to figure out."

Alvin paused and looked around. "Pride is about questioning what everyone else wants us to be like, isn't it? And if we start telling people they can't be there, because they're going through something we haven't gone through, what are we even doing?"

Alvin stood awkwardly for a moment. Then he quickly muttered, "Thank you," before passing the mic to a waiting volunteer.

Alvin saw Daniel had sat back down and crossed his arms. In response, Bree clapped and led the room in applause. Alvin blushed deeply, uncomfortable at being the centre of attention. But he felt seen in a way he hadn't before.

Melissa enveloped him in a tight hug and exclaimed, "That was *awesome!*"

When she released him, Alvin looked over at Rowan. Sure enough, he wore a mischievous grin. "Boyfriend, huh?"

21 You Could Have It So Much Better

"HANDS, OR NO HANDS?"

Alvin thought about Rowan's question for a moment. Then he slipped his hand into Rowan's as an answer and they continued to walk back to school after getting lunch.

Over the last couple months, Alvin and Rowan had fallen into an easy habit of check-ins. Rowan had insisted on maintaining the habit even after letting everyone else know they were together. Alvin had felt silly about it at first — of course they could hold hands if they were dating! But he realized that there were days when he didn't feel like it, and he appreciated being asked. Rowan assured him that he felt the same way. He pointed out that most people probably felt differently from day to day but never got a chance to say so.

"Ugh, stop being so *adorable*," Monica called, her voice full of fake annoyance. Wes and Robyn trailed close behind her as they all headed to class. Just as Rowan had predicted, the school had moved on from gossiping about Alvin's breakup with Alistair after a few weeks. The Trio had gravitated back to Alvin while Alistair was off overachieving.

Rowan squinted at his phone to check the time. "We have a few minutes — what do you want to do? Make fun of Jesse playing soccer?"

Alvin chuckled but shook his head. He pulled Rowan toward the green room. It was musty and cramped, as usual, but with a notable addition. Rowan reached out and poked at the shelf hanging over the couch. He raised his eyebrows questioningly.

"It'll stay up!" Alvin quickly reassured him "I actually got Alistair to hang it. And Robyn to promise not to kick it down."

Alvin rummaged around in his backpack. He pulled out the now dog-eared and worn copy of *The Invisible Orientation* Bree had given him. "I thought . . ." he started. "Well, I've read this already. A few times. And it helped. But I thought we could start, like, a library. For queer kids. Like, I bet there's books you have that you don't need anymore. And maybe . . ."

"Totally!" Rowan exclaimed. "Alvin, that's such a good idea. I have so many things I could bring in."

Alvin held out the book and Rowan took it. He placed it carefully in the centre of the shelf, then turned back to Alvin. He grinned excitedly. "Kiss or no kiss?"

Alvin grinned back and pulled Rowan close.

ACKNOWLEDGEMENTS

The deepest thank you to Kat Mototsune, editor extraordinaire, for the gentle guidance and the occasional check-ins when I hermited too deeply. This story and so many others would not exist without you and your work behind the scenes.

Thank you to my three biggest cheerleaders and emotional support humans — Lauren, Markus, and Tamar. Whether you were double-checking a conversation (at some point during writing all dialogue sounds fake) or refining a point about queer identity or simply reminding me that existence is hard but worth it, you were integral parts of this story. Two of you managed to make your way into the book, and I hope those manifestations are to your liking; the third will have to wait for a future fictional incarnation.

For those who are curious, both Glad Day and LGBT Youth Line are real, and excellent resources for anyone under the LGBTQ2S+ umbrella trying to figure themselves and everything else out.

Glad Day is a little different in our world than in Alvin's, but it's true that it's the oldest surviving LGBTQ2S+ bookstore in the world (and the oldest surviving independent bookstore in Toronto), having been founded in 1970. It remains an integral part of the Village around Church and Wellesley, even as the Village itself becomes increasingly gentrified.

LGBT Youth Line has come a long way from its origin as a phone line for gay and lesbian youth in 1993, now offering text and chat options and hosting a range of queer programming across the province. Their website (youthline.ca) has tons of information on every identity within the LGBTQ2S+ community as well as links to regional organizations with more specific mandates. If you have questions about anything, especially about issues impacting your emotional health, get in touch with them. Too many queer youth suffer in isolation, and organizations like LGBT Youth Line exist so that you don't have to go it alone.

If you or someone you know identifies (or might identify) as asexual, I highly recommend visiting

AVEN (the Asexuality Visibility Education Network — www.asexuality.org), founded in 2001 by David Jay. You can find definitions, FAQs for friends and family, memes, and most importantly — people who can relate to what you're feeling and can help you figure it out. While asexuality has existed for as long as any other sexual orientation, the term only really became popular in the last decade or so, meaning that most people are unfamiliar with the language around it. Asexuality is largely absent from the media and misunderstood by many — hopefully this book can help change that, but you can too by educating yourself and others.